DOUBLE DEAD MAGIC

MAAJA WENTZ

Loon Lake

Editing by: Sara Mack

Cover design: Heather Hamilton-Senter

Double Dead Magic/ Maaja Wentz

ISBN 978-1-7776864-5-1 (Paperback through IS)

ISBN 978-1-7776864-7-5 (Paperback)

ISBN 978-1-7776864-6-8 (Electronic book)

For Gunnar.

1

Priya tipped open her welding visor and stepped back to admire her creation. Two iron rods bent to form muscular legs. The armature looked more like a metal skeleton than a monster, but once she applied the skin, the wicked beast would stand three times her height. *Tyrannosaurus rex* would rise again, the Lizard King of Loon Lake University.

She wiped beads of sweat from her upper lip as sunshine streamed in through the floor-to-ceiling windows, tempting her to walk out to the shore. The cool lake beckoned, but she hated wasting studio time. *First, we work. Then we play.*

Unbelievable.

Staying on at school in June was supposed to release her from Papa's lectures. So why did she hear his favorite sayings in her head? A successful real estate broker, he expected his children to excel in respectable professions. Reluctantly, he had financed Priya's art courses, but she needed to show him it wasn't a mistake. When her creation made headlines back in Toronto, the family would understand the fine arts were legit.

Time to stop woolgathering.

Really? That was another of his expressions. How could she concentrate if she couldn't get Papa's voice out of her head? He was right, though. Studio time was wasting.

Priya turned from the window, just missing a dome of bubbles roiling on the lake's surface.

Later, engrossed in soldering, Priya didn't notice the diving platform floating fifteen feet from shore, or the swimmer balancing there like a twig waiting to be snapped. He waved, unnoticed by the students tossing a Frisbee on the shore, then ran three steps and dove in.

Minutes passed ... too many minutes. A careful observer might have noticed a long stream of bubbles leading deep into the lake but, unfortunately, no one was watching.

Not until the next morning, when the swimmer failed to return, would his roommate suspect something was wrong.

2

Tonya's cramped dorm room didn't have a full-length mirror, so she glanced at her shirt in the communal bathroom while she brushed her teeth. Weakened by magic use, Tonya had been semi-conscious for a month, surviving mostly on liquids. Once her health improved, Loon Lake Council had thrown her in a magic-proof holding cell while they investigated Waldock's so-called murder. With little to do but exercise, and nothing to eat but terrible jail food, Tonya had lost twenty pounds and tossed out most of her clothes.

Her favorite green top was stretchy enough to fit, and wearing it used to give her confidence; it had suited her long red hair. Since death magic turned her locks necro white, a blue top would look better, but by the time she rushed back to her room, grabbed her backpack and found her phone, there was no time to change.

It was her own fault she was late. Tonya had hit snooze on her alarm twice to put off her first class. Then, she'd wasted time deciding between black jeans or blue, as if clothes could stop the gossip. No matter how she looked, the Old Family kids would hate her.

Walking down the Mackenzie residence hallway gave Tonya flashbacks, but summer had transformed the place. Bare walls echoed as students slept off last night's party. In a few hours, they would rise and slip tanned muscles into shorts or sundresses to flirt and laugh their way to class.

But not Tonya.

She waited for the slowest elevator in the world, feeling trapped in this building and very, very late. The sense of desperation triggered a memory of last Halloween, when crowds of drooling food zombies surrounded these walls. Tonya had nearly died to defeat Jack Waldock, but City Council had spelled the non-magical Mundane population to forget what they'd seen, then thrown Tonya into a jail cell. Nice way to thank her.

Her toe tapped the rug. Ten minutes. She might still make it.

Finally, she emerged on the ground floor of her residence and turned left toward the morning hum in the Mackenzie cafeteria. High ceilings and plate-glass windows gave an unobstructed view of Loon Lake, where a kayak glided by in the sunshine. Tonya's stomach growled, but class began in minutes. Like the prison bracelet chafing her left ankle, timely attendance was a condition of parole.

Aromas of bacon and coffee tugged at her empty stomach. Tonya hurried past the tables, zigzagging between milling students. She almost collided with a broad-shouldered hunk with short blonde hair and topaz eyes. He was wearing a high-end camera and a Digital Ninjas t-shirt.

It was Drake!

"Babe!" She waved automatically, then snatched her hand back, ducking into the crowd. She sighed. How her fingers ached to trace those high cheekbones, but that would mean disaster. Drake was off-limits forever.

Had he seen her? Please, please, no. A lump caught in her throat. In the fleeting days between her recovery and the trial, he had become her first boyfriend. Sweet moments lost forever. In this case, literally.

If Drake remembered her, Ashton Security would wipe his memory a second time, and repeating the spell would damage his brain.

3

Tonya's parole officer, Miranda, had sketched her a map to class and even sympathized with her plight. Every member of the Old Families knew the conditions of her parole—remedial magic lessons.

They taught magic in University College, a relic of the 1800s assembled from red sandstone blocks. Leaded windows bubbled with age across the front of the rectangular building that was book-ended by two towers. Gargoyles peered over the eves in a cloudless sky, waterspouts empty but willing to douse passersby when it rained.

Tonya entered through a stone archway. The hallways ran across the front and along two sides of a manicured lawn surrounded by covered arcades. If she wasn't late, she might have grabbed a coffee from the café sheltered by the covered walkway and sunned herself in the green space. It would be nice to pretend she was there to get a normal degree like the Mundane students from non-magical families.

Instead, she took the right-hand hallway and hurried past oak-paneled walls and stone stairs worn by centuries of student feet. To find her special class, she'd have to go farther.

Tucked behind the impressive oak panels of the hallway, she knew the lecture rooms to be small and shabbily renovated. The plastic seats were uncomfortably modern, with fold-down arms instead of desks. Tonya had started a suffocating first-year English class in one of them. She hoped the magic lecture room was larger.

Ashton Security would have approved the tiny rooms with leaded windows and cramped chairs to restrain Tonya's movement. Add the ankle monitor and constant surveillance of strangers, and Loon Lake University felt like another prison. The City Council had tasked Professor Kirkdene with taming Tonya's powers. He would surely report her tardiness to Ashton Security.

With her shoulders back and chest out, she strode like she had plenty of time and knew exactly where she was going. Never let them see you sweat.

Wait.

She had followed the directions perfectly, right down to the room number, so why was she facing a dead end?

"Tonya? I barely recognized you with white hair." Arjun caught up on lanky legs, his shiny black locks flowing past his shoulders.

"What are you doing here?"

"Summer school. You?" A smile crossed his lips like he was in on a joke.

Arjun was a Digital Ninja like Drake. He had witnessed the same food-crazy carnage as her boyfriend, so why hadn't Ashton Security wiped his memory?

"I think you already know. What are you taking?"

"Guess." He held up paper directions similar to hers. His grin explained everything. He was from Toronto, but out-of-towners sometimes absorbed enough Loon Lake magic to develop powers.

"Looks like we're both lost." She pointed to the dead end dominated by a glass case crowded with tarnished plaques and silver trophies.

"And late."

He was hiding secrets behind those deep brown eyes. "Why do you need summer school?" she asked.

"I'm a keener. What year are you in?"

"I'm starting first year for the second time. You know that." It felt like everyone did.

Arjun looked from the display case to his hand-drawn map. "This is the right spot."

"Can I see your map?"

Before he could hand it over, the surrounding air shimmered, the display case disappeared, and Marta Ashton appeared in a darkened entrance. Small and pretty, like a viper, Marta had singled out Tonya for punishment in her first year. What nasty twist of fate threw them together in summer school? No professor would dare fail Donna Ashton's daughter, so she should be on vacation.

"Hey, dummies! Don't stand there till the end of Tonya's parole. Get in here!"

4

Arjun and Tonya entered a wooden elevator. Tonya's stomach rose as they dropped. Was it safe to travel in an oversized packing crate? Through gaps between the boards, aged timber and marble flashed by until they sank beneath the building.

"Are you excited?" Marta beamed at Arjun.

Her first-year nemesis hadn't changed. She had the same long dark hair and ruddy lips. The same diver's body and Napoleon complex. The prison bracelet digging into her ankle would cause Tonya less pain than Marta.

"You need to know a few things." Marta's eyes sparkled, delighted to impress Arjun with her superior knowledge. "Three kinds of Old Families built Loon Lake, but only Mods are cool. We study magic and believe in using it openly. Pures are uptight goody goodies who have magical ability but never use it. Trads are hypocrites who practice magic but never in front of Mundanes."

"Like me."

"No, you're a Mod now. Your ability is soaking up Loon Lake magic, but it will take time to discover your powers." Marta tried to throw an arm around Arjun's wide shoulders but was too short, so she put a hand on his arm. She quirked her head at Tonya and whispered loudly, "Watch out for fakes like her. She says she's a Pure—but she's done worse magic than any of us."

Tonya inhaled slowly through her nose. Old Family factions and their stupid rules. If it were up to Tonya, everyone would use magic.

Too bad the only thing Mods, Trads, and Pures agreed on was that Tonya deserved punishment. It wasn't fair. The only time Tonya had used her powers was in the fight against a dangerous revenant, Jack Waldock. To show their infinite gratitude, the City Council held a tribunal and charged her with unlawful magic use.

Ignorant busybodies.

But that was Loon Lake for you—rules, rules, tradition, and politics. Poor Arjun was stepping on a hornet's nest.

With a shudder, the elevator sank to the bottom floor and opened into a dark corridor hewn from raw earth. Without reinforcement, how did it not collapse? Tonya reached out to feel the wall, but Marta grabbed her wrist.

"No touching." She grinned. "You're still officially a Pure, remember? This is Mod and Trad territory. If the hallway senses an intruder, it might bury you."

"You're not serious."

Marta chuckled.

"What about me?" Arjun hesitated, staring at the ceiling.

"Don't worry." Marta put her arm through Arjun's. "From now on, you're with us."

5

At noon in the Mackenzie cafeteria, Drake found his dark-haired roommate lined up at the steam tables. It was hard to miss Zain's startled-hedgehog hairstyle.

"Deep-fried sponge in red syrup is not Chinese food." Zain scowled as the lunch lady doled out heaps of fried rice.

"If you don't like the food, why ask to meet me here?"

"Spoilers."

Drake picked up a tray. "It smells good."

"But it's false advertising."

June light streamed in through the wall of glass facing the lake, warming Drake's face. Students sat in plastic chairs eating burgers, fries, burritos, and pizza. "It's a cafeteria serving cafeteria food."

"The sign says Chinese." Zain pointed to steam trays of deep-fried chicken balls, egg rolls, and fried rice. "There aren't enough vegetables to garnish a plate."

With her head down, the server dished Zain's food as quickly as possible.

"Where's the Moo Shu pork? Where's the Beijing Duck?"

"In China, so unless you have a plane ticket ..."

"I will once I'm a big Hollywood director."

Drake smiled at the server. "Fried rice, please." He was hungry, and Zain was starting to steam his vegetables. His friend insisted they stay in residence all summer to work on a movie, but so far Zain had turned down every actor Drake suggested.

On the way to a table, Zain froze. "Finally. That's the perfect girl," he whispered.

An athletic beauty lined up at the omelet station. Freckles sprinkled her flawless brown complexion, and gold gloss shimmered on her lips.

"We must get her before they make her the next Bond girl."

"Grace? She reminds me of Kat Graham."

"As in Bonnie Bennett? Wait! You admit to watching *Vampire Diaries*? Not cool, Drake. Think of your reputation."

"What reputation?"

"Purveyor of high-test horror and classy things that go bump in the night."

"That's you. I'm in it for the cinematography."

Grace glanced their way, and Zain darted behind Drake. "Ahh! She saw me."

She regarded them with clear green eyes.

Drake stepped forward, gesturing toward Zain. "Excuse my friend. He never leaves the editing suite."

"Er, hi?" Zain's voice quavered.

When she turned back to the omelet station, Zain whispered, "Grace is perfect. Willowy but muscular enough to outrun the monster."

"Can she act?" Drake asked.

"Don't you remember? We saw her in the campus production of *A Christmas Carol*."

Drake nodded. A cap and nightgown had hidden her braids and curves, but her expressive face had shone through. "I loved her Scrooge. What a transformation!"

"When she saw Morley's ghost, her scream was perfect. Help me?"

Zain offered him a pleading look, and Drake knew how much this movie meant to his friend.

Drake joined Grace at the omelet station. "I'm Drake, and this is Zain. Do you have a sec?"

She shrugged at the line in front of her. "I'm Grace."

Zain puffed out his chest. "We know. So, are you busy this weekend?"

Wide-eyed, Grace looked from Zain back to Drake. "You both want a date?"

"We saw you in *A Christmas Carol*," said Zain. "You. Were. Breathtaking."

"Thanks."

"Christmas puts me in the mood for horror." Zain grinned.

"What?"

"Except you should have gone with a beard. What kind of Scrooge doesn't have a beard?"

Grace sighed theatrically. "I asked for a beard, but the director refused."

Zain smiled back. "Wanna star in our film?"

She made a face. "What kind of film?"

"We're still writing the ..." Zain looked at Drake.

"The best horror movie ever. *Cabin in the Woods* meets *Blair Witch Project*."

Zain put on a cheesy Transylvanian accent. "Join us. Ve vant to make you famous!"

"A vampire movie?" Grace raised an eyebrow. "That won't get me into Juilliard."

"Better. A summer vacation scream fest," said Zain. The line edged forward. "An artist friend is building a monster. Once you see it, you'll beg to star in this film."

"Do I get paid?" Grace's turn came, so she ordered at the counter.

"Even better." Zain trailed after her. "We'll make you a celebrity."

"Or make me look like a fool." She took her food to the cashier.

Drake fell in beside her. "You'll share the profits."

"As in one third of nothing equals nothing?" She tried to look annoyed, but her eyes lingered on Drake's face.

"As in 20% of a movie so awesome they'll distribute it everywhere equals your big break." Zain smiled tightly.

Grace took a meal card out of her purse. "I don't know. I'm busy with school and auditions."

Zain's face fell.

"Relax," Drake whispered to Zain. "I got this." He handed the cashier his card. "The project is worth thinking about." He nudged Grace's arm. "Let me buy you lunch?"

6

Tonya followed Marta along a dark corridor that opened into a large underground cavern. Students gathered around Professor Kirkdene, a deeply tanned elder in a plaid shirt, undershirt, faded jeans, and a green cap. His powerful shoulders and relaxed stance brought to mind a local farmer pausing in his work to have a chat. He was nothing like Tonya had expected in a professor of magic, but she wasn't disappointed. Above his head floated a glowing orb bright enough to illuminate the room in bluish light.

His lips moved, and he gestured lazily as he spoke to a deep ring of students. Unable to hear from the back, Tonya jostled forward ignoring the Mods' dirty looks.

"We will conduct our experiments here."

Experiments? Tonya always thought families handed down spells in grimoires.

A red-faced student in khakis and a pink polo shirt raised his hand.

"Yes, Jobson?"

"How are we going to be evaluated?"

"First survive, then work on getting an A." Kirkdene's icy blue eyes gleamed. Maybe he wasn't kidding.

His nasty look triggered a memory. Moving through the huddle of students, she got a better view of his face. Unbelievable.

Professor Kirkdene had sicced his dog on her through a cornfield in October and helped the Ashtons capture her. That explained Marta's glee. Tonya's stomach fluttered. If the professor failed her, the City Council would never restore her powers.

The group followed him single file through a narrow passage, the musty smell of the rocks filling their nostrils. The corridor widened into a finished hallway with tiled flooring. Their footsteps echoed as they passed between marble niches and mausoleums. The inscriptions memorialized Loon Lakers from the eighteenth and early nineteenth centuries, and the funerary carvings ranged from stone angels to realistic portraits of terrifying hags. Everything from pumpkins and cats to owls and black bears graced the tombs. No ordinary symbols for Tonya's ancestors! Fascinated by the carvings, she almost forgot what they represented.

Until they stopped in front of a pile of age-stained skulls.

When had the booming population of Loon Lake died so quickly that they needed to stack the skeletons? There was no record of bubonic plague in southern Ontario.

"This is your heritage," Kirkdene announced. "The Old Families brought these bones from Europe." He addressed Tonya directly. "That is how magic works for the Old Families. Power accumulates in crypts and cemeteries passed into the living like an inheritance. Did they explain that in your Pure family?"

"Uh, not exactly."

The students tittered.

What Tonya had meant to say was she'd picked up this information at school. It wasn't a secret among the Old Families, and she wasn't ignorant. She chewed a fingernail, then stopped herself. He'd made her look foolish on her first day. So what? The professor was just another Mod, happy to see her punished.

This summer was going to be awful, but it was nothing compared to battling food zombies and surviving a near-coma state. She wasn't the naïve and protected girl she'd been last September. For two months, she could withstand almost anything.

Marta and Kirkdene led the way and she followed behind, suddenly conscious that thousands of pounds of granite and limestone rested on the ceiling. With the words of a spell and a small sacrifice, any of these Mods could create a rockfall or collapse.

Abruptly, white-tiled floors and walls ushered in a modern addition to the catacombs. A prickling sensation stirred Tonya's neck and shoulders. Despite herself, she glanced back, feeling like she was being watched. Jobson trailed behind her, peering in every direction. At least she wasn't the only one creeped out by the hallways under City Hall.

Progressing at Kirkdene's laid-back pace, they passed evenly spaced iron doors with barred windows. The anklet on Tonya's left leg sparked against her skin. Something tugged on her powers, then the sensation vanished.

Weird. Sensing life force was passive for Tonya, and living things surrounded them. The dirt housed millions of insects and hundreds of little critters, each pulsing with a tiny green aura.

From the moment her parole officer slapped the magic-sensing anklet on her, she had contained her ability to drain and manipulate life energy. It had been a small but constant effort, but to get caught using her powers would be to lose them forever.

But here? Tonya shivered. It was as if all those tiny flames of life had guttered out. She sensed nothing.

Moments before, she had felt the life force in each student, but that ability had gone dark. The prison cells on either side must suppress magic. Why had Kirkdene taken students of magic to the one place their powers wouldn't work?

At the surface lay City Hall, whose councilors controlled the Old Family Tribunal. They were about to pass beneath the council chamber where they had convicted her. A few steps ahead sat the cell where Tonya had spent a month awaiting trial. Could there be a more humiliating way to start class?

"We're directly below City Hall." Kirkdene stared at Tonya. "Any of you been here before?"

Everybody knew about her arrest. When no other student reacted, she raised her hand.

Circling behind Tonya, Marta snickered and whispered to the other students. Tonya turned and whispered back, "Really mature. What are you, still in high school?"

Kirkdene cleared his throat. "What makes these cells special?"

Hunched, Jobson glanced back over his shoulder. "They're full of ghosts."

"We built Loon Lake on ghost power. Can any of you be more specific?"

The Mods looked to Marta, awaiting her okay before replying, but she raised her chin, too cool to cooperate.

The silent pause stretched. "Ashton Security unearthed something special." Kirkdene's icy eyes glowed against his bronzed face. "Come."

The hallway opened into a white tiled dome-shaped cavern, lit by Kirkdene's glowing orb. In a niche set high into the farthest wall, a staff extended, mounted like a torch in a castle.

"The Staff of Storms. We thought it was just a legend until this spring when I unearthed it in a field north of town. After 200 plus years in the ground, the wood should be rotten, but power protects it."

Half-expecting lightning and thunder, Tonya gazed up at six feet of polished hardwood topped by an enormous amethyst set in gold.

The legendary artifact set off a chain reaction of chatter.

"How much is the jewel worth?"

"I wanna touch it."

"The style looks so 1970s."

"When can we leave? Inhaling dead people dust makes my nose run."

Ignoring their comments, Kirkdene prompted, "Who can tell me what the Staff of Storms does?"

The conversation hushed and the students avoided Kirkdene's gaze.

Marta stood tall. "If no one else knows, I'll say it. Ashton Security uses it to siphon away criminal powers, so freaks like Tonya and her mother don't lose control and suck the life force out of everyone."

Tonya swallowed and took a deep breath, but she had to put her hands in her pockets so they wouldn't shake. The others smiled at Marta's attack on her. One gave Marta a high five.

Tonya's stomach did a little flip, but she kept her expression neutral. *Never let them see you sweat.* All she had to do was pass this wretched summer course. That was the deal. Earn the credit to satisfy her parole and get her powers back. Nothing Marta could do would make Tonya mess that up. All the Pure families, including her adoptive parents, had rejected her. But with powers, she could still have something.

However, there comes a time when deep breathing and all the meditation techniques she had practiced in prison couldn't hold back the wave of rejection. Their hostile faces and Marta's superior grin choked her up. Sometimes she would trade anything—powers, her school year, friends, even knowing Helen was her birth mother, to turn back the clock and live as she did before Halloween.

September had been the happiest month of her life. Priya was her new best friend, and Drake had just started flirting.

"Slowpoke, aren't you coming?" Marta goaded from the front of the pack. Beside her, Arjun didn't object.

After ambling throughout the class, Kirkdene suddenly sped up, long legs swinging. Tonya could never get past the mob of students ahead. The professor rushed on and on until the floor began slanting upward. As the air warmed, it carried the sweet scent of fresh cut grass and flowers. They emerged into a storage room filled with plants, sacks of fertilizer, and hoses. Through a door, they spilled into the huge greenhouse that dominated the City Hall Gardens.

Surrounded by students, Kirkdene lectured them about Loon Lake's history and the founding Old Families. With a smile and wave to passing citizens visiting the greenhouse, he mentioned the private collection of Old Family documents in City Hall. Around her, Tonya felt the students shift from foot to foot or whisper to their neighbors, bored. Even Tonya knew about the concealed Old Family library and Loon Lake's City Council, composed of Old Family counselors sworn to carry out Mundane and magical business. If only the Mundanes knew their city was run on two levels: the ordinary, which was visible to them, and the magical, with meetings in a second council chamber hidden behind a door they could not see.

When Tonya was growing up, her adopted mother, Barbara, was a dedicated Pure. Her father, Jim, grew up in a Mundane family with no knowledge of magic. Yet nothing Kirkdene said was news to Tonya. When would Kirkdene teach them something useful, like how to cast a spell?

He wound up his lecture with homework readings from a grimoire Tonya had never heard of.

"Excuse me, professor, but where can I buy a grimoire?"

A few students laughed.

"Every family has one."

"Not mine."

"If there is no tradition of magic in your family, start with an empty notebook and learn by observation."

"Can't I borrow one from the library?"

"Are you asking if the City Librarian will entrust you with a centuries-old record of our magical heritage?"

Marta stifled a laugh behind Kirkdene's back.

It would have been nice if Arjun said something, but he just stood there, staring at Tonya as if seeing her for the first time.

Kirkdene marched the class across manicured lawns and between flowerbeds, stopping in front of a dented pickup truck. A bumpy load lay hidden under a tarp in the back. "I need a pair of volunteers."

Jobson stepped forward followed by Arjun.

From behind, Tonya whispered to Arjun, "Don't you want to know what it's for?"

When Kirkdene glanced at his vehicle, the group shifted back, leaving her beside Arjun.

"Okay, Tonya, Arjun, pile in." Kirkdene's smile deepened his wrinkles.

Jobson's face flushed. "What about me?"

A light breeze dispersed a nasty whiff from under the tarp. "Trust me, you're not missing much."

7

Arjun climbed into the cab beside Professor Kirkdene, taking half the seat. Tonya crammed in beside him on the window side. She had to lean into Arjun to close the door. He smiled. They were acquaintances in the Digital Ninjas, because he was Priya's friend. In the catacombs, he'd stood by Marta and never once defended Tonya, but now he chatted animatedly as if they were BFFs. *Buddy, make up your mind.*

Choking on rank odors from the flatbed, Tonya hit the window button and let the wind ruffle her hair.

"Almost there." Kirkdene floored it.

Good. Manure fumes and Arjun's mixed signals were torture. But she had no choice. This was her chance to win over Kirkdene. Once she showed him what a hard worker she was, he'd have to relent and let her use her powers.

Wouldn't he?

They drove east to the limits of town and then sped north, slowed, then turned east again onto a faded two-lane highway. On either side, fields of young corn and pumpkin blossoms flew by, reminders of last Halloween. Despite the heat, Tonya shivered.

"Where are we going?" Arjun asked.

"I keep a farm near here. We have chickens, goats, and a donkey to scare the coyotes. I grow organic garlic and wildflowers for honey, which is where you come in. I need help to spread the honey." He thumbed back at his cargo.

"If that's honey," Tonya said, "cows have black and yellow stripes."

"And bees say moo." Arjun laughed.

How much longer until she could get away from that "honey?" It felt like the stench was soaking into her clothes. They'd smell it on her when she went back to the dorm.

Fifteen very long minutes later, they turned between twin maples onto a gravel laneway. Gravel crackled under the tires all the way to a red brick farmhouse with a shiny steel roof.

Beside it stood a weathered gray barn that was missing several upright boards. They had branded the year 1810 over the gaping door. The bottom sheltered cows, and the second floor supported an unused hayloft. These days, harvesters rolled hay into wheels wrapped in white plastic, which were left on the fields like enormous cheeses.

The moment the truck stopped, Tonya leaped out and took a deep breath of fresh air. Bad mistake. Extra fresh manure smell filled her nose and made her cough until her eyes watered.

Beside Arjun, Kirkdene looked shorter than he had in the tunnels. From the flatbed, he snatched a pair of shovels. "You see that mound of cow flaps around the feeding station?"

Tonya wished she couldn't. A handful of cows stood ankle-deep in a pond of liquid manure.

"Yes." Arjun winced.

"Shovel it into the flatbed, and then we'll spread it over the garlic field."

"You can't make us do that." Arjun protested. "We're your students."

He answered with his eyes on Tonya. "Participation is voluntary, but I have a lot of friends in this town."

Arjun gasped, then started to gag and cough.

"You expect me to do it by hand?" It would take Tonya a week.

"Don't worry. You can both get extra credit for using magic."

"So, you'll take my anklet off?" Relief surged through her. He'd let her use her powers!

"Not a chance, jailbird."

8

ROBERTO ACCEPTED THE GLASS Madre held out to him and polished it with a tea towel. One more concession to her grandiose plan. *Didn't they already have enough money?*

He belonged with his friends in the cafés and shops of Miraflores or surfing at Punta Negra. At home, in Peru, he could surf every day, and nobody treated him like a waiter. He was used to a car and driver, posh nightclubs, and hanging with prep school friends. Loon Lake didn't have one Michelin-starred restaurant. Caramba! A man of his talents wasn't meant to serve at the pastry counter like one of Madre's minions.

The Condor Bakery. You would think they could choose something more original, but that was Madre and Papi. They were not subtle. They fooled nobody with their humble act, sending the regular employees home. His mother had asked the Ashtons to tea, then fussed around as if Donna was the Queen of Spain. It was embarrassing.

With a jingle of bells over the door, Donna Ashton strode in, followed by Marta and her brothers, Marvin and Stephen Jr. "Nice paint job." Donna nodded at a mural of condors flying over the Andes. "Much better than the dusty Scottish tea towels that used to clutter up the place."

Papi smiled. "Come in. Sit." He pulled out a café chair that still had a plaid cushion left over from the previous owners. Cheap as porridge, his parents had snapped up the Scottish Bakery when the former owners retired to Glasgow.

Flexing bulging muscles, Junior set two tables together. Roberto went to help. With a wrist flick, he applied a handloomed tablecloth decorated with stripes and geometric llamas. Once the Ashton family sat, Madre lifted her index finger at Roberto. "Tea!"

He didn't object. Madre knew best if you knew what was good for you. Like a good little waiter, he went behind the pastry counter to boil the kettle. His parents had kept the Scottish teapot collection to placate elderly Loon Lakers used to drinking afternoon tea. Madre switched out clotted cream and scones for empanadas and alfajores cookies filled with dulce de leche. The old dears whined about the changes but still turned up regularly.

"No tea for me. I need a milkshake." Marta smirked.

"Sorry. How about iced tea?" Roberto asked. It was a bakery, not a burger joint.

"Whatever."

Let her try to annoy him. Madre's pastries, a special family recipe, would give him revenge. The Ashtons were to eat the pastries Madre put aside. Roberto smiled as he filled the kettle. Donna Ashton and her brothers could scheme all they liked, but they'd never outwit Madre.

He would never admit it to his surf buddies back in Lima, but Roberto enjoyed the ritual of heating the teapot and the scent of boiling water hitting fresh tea leaves. It was soothing—when he wasn't forced to serve Marta. She was pretending not to recognize him. Little witch.

Was she still freaked out by the way Waldock had taken over his body in October? Binging on pancakes with Lynette, driving over a bumpy field, lying beneath the Three-Century Ash to let the Entity absorb them, body and mind. He remembered snippets with big gaps in his memory. Nightmares had haunted him for weeks, but she should be over it. In fact, she didn't spare Roberto a second glance, despite his devastating good looks. Weirder still, she sat across the table from her oldest brother, her face animated, drinking in every word.

Roberto didn't understand it.

Big brother Marvin wore a striped white dress shirt accessorized by a chewed pencil over one ear. What a nerd. Stephen Jr. had a boring brush cut, but his red Quicksilver shirt bulged with muscles as he strode to the pastry case. Stephen was tall enough to look down at Roberto as he blurted, "Can I get a hot dog?"

"These have meat." Roberto loaded up a platter with Madre's charmed empanadas.

In his surfer shirt, Stephen Jr. looked like Roberto's social equal—but a hot dog? How cheap. And that disappointed little boy look when he didn't get one? His family might wield power in Loon Lake, but Junior was a loser.

At the table, Donna and Marvin put their heads together, chatting with Madre. Before long, their eyes went glassy, and their mouths gaped. Too bad Marta had refused the special pastries. Typical girl. Probably worried about her weight. But even without spells, she would give in to Madre. People always did.

He slid the platter of baked goods directly in front of Marta, and the enticing aromas jabbed at Roberto's stomach. Madre's recipes never lost their appeal, with or without magic.

Donna's proud coiffe encircled her face like a black mane. Crumbs clung to the corner of her mouth, and she almost purred, "It's nice to see newcomers settling in."

"We have your beautiful little city to thank," said Papi. "There's something in the air."

"You're not kidding," said Junior. "The previous owners left this bakery after a ghost moved into the back room."

"Junior!" Marta exclaimed.

"Show respect." Marvin waved his pencil at him.

"There's more here than ghosts." Madre spread her hands on the table and tipped her head up, eyes closed, as she inhaled deeply. "I could sense the power of this place all the way from Peru."

"Is that right?" Donna beamed.

"And since last October, it's gotten stronger." Marvin chewed his pencil.

"Which is why we invited you. It's good to know our neighbors, and since the unfortunate demise of Jack Waldock "

A cloud crossed Donna's face, but she kept her smile fixed on Madre who continued. "We were wondering how we can help."

Marta twisted in her chair, probably dying to unleash her sarcasm, until Marvin narrowed his eyes at her.

With a nail file, Donna smoothed her red talons. "What do you propose?"

9

IT WAS PAST NOON when Priya woke, slumped over the drawing board. Her head ached where it rested on sweat-damp glass, and it swam with last night's dreams. Behind closed eyelids, thunder crashed, and lightning illuminated a beast. Its enormous heart thundered as it swayed to its feet, extinct no more.

This was a job for coffee. Lots and lots of coffee. Priya hoped a hot shower would slough off the weird visions, but when she closed her eyes under the showerhead, the scaley monster wouldn't fade from her mind.

Her eyes popped open, and she shivered under the spray like a wet cat. Mere stupidity. No reason to worry. It was just her imagination, no matter how real the dream felt. Sometimes being an artist wasn't as fun as it seemed.

Two rounds of shampoo and a rinse with conditioner put the nightmares out of mind. Toweling off, she stood in front of her tiny dormitory closet. Black gothy goodness hung to the left. Jeans, paint-spattered smocks, and workout clothes hung to the right. Back home, a third section held traditional wear, but here the fanciest thing she owned was a pencil skirt and blouse for job interviews.

The forecast was hot for June. She chose a short, black lace skirt and a flattering bias-cut top. You never knew who you might bump into on campus. After class, she'd continue her summer job hunt. She had been searching since April and had dropped off a dozen resumes without a call back. It was a matter of pride. Her family was paying her tuition, but she had to buy extra materials for her creations. How could she show Papa receipts for her masterpiece when she was still figuring out what it was?

Her dreams whispered that she'd created a monster, but what made her shiver with delight was the sensation of commanding life and death. Amid thunder and lightning, she had risen akin to Victor Frankenstein, looming over the slab, animating her creature—like a god.

That must be her dream's inspiration. She had studied Mary Shelley's *Frankenstein* for Women's Studies. And there were many parallels between herself and Victor. Her sculpting was a secret kept from her family. She toiled at night, bringing art to life that would shock and inspire. Parents and siblings scoffed at her aspirations, but she would show them. This was the sign that proved her vocation. It had to be.

All this time, she thought she was toiling over a T. Rex, but dinosaurs belonged in little kid dreams. Her vision beast meant so much more. She would give it wings.

10

DISGUSTING SLOP ROLLED OFF their shovels. At least the professor had provided rubber boots.Tonya stood ankle deep in stench and shoveled up liquid sewage, but it oozed off her shovel before she could walk it to the truck.

"You've got to be kidding." Arjun watched her from the edge of the mire.

Kirkdene didn't scold Arjun for standing idly. In fact, he joined him, observing Tonya's fruitless efforts.

"How's that working for ya?" The professor crossed his arms.

The man was toying with her. At first, Tonya had worked to prove she was no sore loser and willing to learn, even from her enemies. But there was no winning him over. After the heat, the smell, and student laughter at her expense, Tonya had had it. She waded away from the mire, ready to leave.

Kirkdene slipped into his own boots and motioned her to follow him into the barn. "You can use magic, but there's always a cost. Most times, it's cheaper to pay for the electricity." He hauled a pump into the middle of the manure puddle, spooking cows who headed for drier ground.

"There." He switched on the pump, which spewed liquid manure through a ten-foot hose. "I'll let the two of you figure out getting it onto the truck." Without waiting for an answer, he went into the farmhouse.

Arjun approached the wet end and toed it with his boots. "Turn it off."

Tonya found the switch on the side of the pump and waited for Arjun to the thread the hose between the tarp and the tailgate. "Ready?"

Arjun backed away.

"Hold onto it. It's going to spray all over."

Arjun held up his hands. "No way am I standing anywhere near that thing when it starts to spew."

"Don't be a baby." Tonya shouldered him out of the way and grabbed the hose, aiming it at the center of the flatbed. "Go turn it on."

He hesitated. It was the first time Tonya had seen anyone tiptoe in rubber boots, but Arjun finally reached the pump and switched it on. After that, it took some coaxing to get him to move the heavy pump from puddle to puddle, but he came through in the end.

An hour later, Tonya was sweaty, dirty, and covered in muck.

"Finished." Arjun was mud spattered, but mostly clean from the waist up.

Without a word, Tonya raced him to the house where a length of hose hung next to the kitchen garden. Beating him to the faucet, Tonya turned on the water and adjusted the nozzle to high pressure. It felt great to let the cold spray clear the muck off her arms and legs.

Arjun took off his boots, socks, shirt, pants ... "Gimme that."

Tonya wasn't ready to relinquish the hose. She turned it on Arjun, who held out muscled arms and braced against the icy flow, laughing.

She had rinsed her manure off but still felt dirty. What she wouldn't give for fresh clothes and a bar of soap.

"Mine!" Arjun snatched the hose out of her hands and turned it on her, forcing her to turn her back to the chilly spray.

When she'd gotten clean a second time, Arjun carried his shirt but put on his pants to get back in the truck.

Tonya's hair was still damp when Kirkdene dropped Arjun in front of Mackenzie Hall. She waved goodbye, but he didn't look back. Really? After what they'd suffered together, he couldn't spare her a goodbye? She would never understand why Priya called him a friend.

As the truck crawled through campus, Tonya tucked her head behind her arm and crunched down in her seat, hoping not to be seen.

"Please, Professor, could you drop me at the Western Gate?" She dreaded running into any Mods without a proper shower. If Marta saw her bedraggled hair and wet clothes, she'd guess what Tonya had been doing and tease her for weeks.

"I have to grade papers." When the truck pulled up to the curb, Tonya bolted away from campus, vowing to never approach another cow. Her sprint slowed to a training pace, and by the time she passed through the Western Gate, she strolled. Arms wide to the air, Tonya let the piney breezes dry her clothes in the sun. Away from the farm, life force pulsed at her from every tree and critter. Under City Hall, and again in his truck, Kirkdene had been dampening her magical abilities.

That had to be it. On their own, Tonya's powers reached out and sensed life from all directions. They yearned to tap life force from nature, but actively using her powers would trigger her ankle bracelet. For now, it was enough to sense that forbidden energy and promise herself that once her parole ended, she could use it again.

Beside the highway, gravel crunched underfoot, and her shoes squelched with water. Wind batted damp white hair into her face on her way north to Helen's place. She wanted to tell her birth mother she'd survived her first class with the Mods. Arjun was a jerk, but at least he remembered who she was.

If only it could have been Drake.

She couldn't afford to think about him. Walking along the roadside past charred tree trunks gave Tonya a pang. In the fight against a deadly, subterranean Entity, she had burned down the cemetery. Flames had spread to Helen's Herbal Healing Shop, demolishing her home above the store.

Was it any wonder Tonya was an outcast? Everything she touched combusted.

Her parents had divorced and sold their home while Tonya was recovering in Helen's trailer. Dad had moved to his new home in Toronto, but visited Tonya in jail and helped her move into her dorm room when she got out.

Mom had taken an apartment on the fringes of Loon Lake City and spoke only to fellow Pures. She had to shun Tonya, or the Pures would cast her out. Most mothers would have chosen their daughter over their political affiliations, but Mom blocked Tonya's number and pretended she was dead.

Maybe her adopted mother had never fully accepted her. When Mom found out Dad was visiting their daughter, she made him choose between Tonya and herself. That had backfired. Tonight, Dad would call for an update on today's magical training. On the weekend, she'd take the bus to Toronto and visit him.

She loved her parents, but it was a relief to walk alone beside the highway, away from the drama. The strong sunshine cheered her despite her proximity to the cemetery. Since the fire, its blackened tree stumps stabbed her with guilt. Helen should never have forgiven her, but she did.

As she reached the wrought-iron fence, a little boy trailed after her, taunting in a whiny singsong:

Tonya Turncoat went to jail
For making Waldock very pale.
They let her out for good behavior
Forgetting how she killed her neighbor.
How can one who burns our tree,
And desecrates the cemetery,
Harp upon her innocence?
Tonya Turncoat makes no sense!

Before he could start another verse, she turned on him. "Go away!"

Unafraid, he dodged and wove, staying just out of reach. "Nah, nah! Can't catch me! Better stay out of the cemetery!"

She gave chase. Felt stupid. Stopped.

The child skipped away, laughing and singing louder than before.

Tonya sighed. "Who taught you that song?"

"Wouldn't you like to know?"

A modern bully would troll her online, not teach kids hurtful songs. Or rather, one peculiar kid. He wore shorts with leather shoes, a vest, and a jacket. His newsboy cap glowed with a misty aura.

The little ghost loaded a slingshot, pulled back, and fired it at her. Too late to duck, she put up her hands to protect her forehead.

His ammo passed through her fingers, but she didn't feel it. The ghost had shot a phantom stone. She found it on the grass behind her, glowing faintly, solid as a wisp of fog.

"Nice try, kid. Sticks and stones may break my bones, but runty ghosts will never hurt me."

His baby face crumpled as he faded away leaving her completely alone.

All her friends had been magically spelled to forget her. Mods, Trads, Pures, and Mom had turned their backs.

She yearned for the good times with Drake and Priya and the Digital Ninjas, but the City Council had barred her from seeing them forever. The prison anklet and her solitude were turning her hometown into a prison.

It wasn't right, and she swore to make City Council give her another chance.

11

WHEN ASHTON SECURITY TOOK Tonya into custody, Helen was living in a rented trailer behind the burned remains of her store. She had paid contractors to haul away the wreckage and replaced it with a trimmed lawn and tidy flower beds. In the rush to start classes immediately after her release, Tonya hadn't yet met up with Helen.

Set behind a freshly paved parking lot, the new Herbal Healing Shop drew Tonya's eye up three stories of mirrored glass. How could Helen have afforded such expensive renovations?

Heaviness filled her stomach. Had Helen sold the store? Lately, a rash of for-sale signs speckled Loon Lake, but the shop was more than Helen's livelihood. Serving the community with her charms and cures—even when it broke the rules—was Helen's calling. Tonya couldn't imagine her in any other job.

She rushed in the door where rows of shelves divided a bright, high-ceilinged space. "Helen? Anyone here?" She strode across the front of the store, looking down each aisle for customers or staff.

Empty.

Everything looked too clean, modern, and antiseptic. Medicine smells from cough syrup-sweet to bitter and sour invaded her nose. Bottles of vitamins and supplements stood beside makeup displays. The white walls and packaged goods looked too clinical.

Shortly after giving Tonya her first summer job, Helen had taught her to avoid electricity because it leached power out of herbal magic. They had used a manual treadle sewing machine to sew sachets for remedies and charms. It was sweaty work without air-conditioning, but laughter filled that log cabin long before Tonya discovered Helen was her birth mother. Sometimes remembering that summer filled her with nostalgia, but months in prison had given Tonya time to see things clearly.

On her own, Helen could charm animals and influence people. Together, they could channel power, allowing Helen to cheat death and destroy Waldock but at the price of Tonya's health.

Before that battle, Tonya would have done anything for Helen. But the florescent lights, junk food aisle, and rows of over-the-counter meds made her wonder. Her birth mother was the ultimate nature girl. Why build a commercial drugstore hostile to nature and magic?

Overhead, something heavy dragged along the ceiling towards the back of the store. Following the sound, Tonya slipped behind a counter completely unlike the antique one in the old shop that used to hold weird-smelling preserves, unguents, and healing oils.

A door on the back wall led to a narrow metal staircase. On the second floor, Tonya hauled open a fire door. Wow.

Helen had replaced her modest 1940s-era apartment with one enormous living space. The entryway opened directly into a high-ceilinged room with a stone fireplace against the far wall. L-shaped leather couches divided out a living area in the center, with rugs and seating surrounding the hearth.

To the right side of the couches stood a dining room table with a modern china cabinet and a sideboard. Underfoot, polished barn board harmonized with a rustic chandelier hung from the ceiling, which was ringed with bannisters overlooking the room from the top floor.

To the left stood an open kitchen with marble counters, a generous island with cutting board, and cabinets in shades of oak and blue stain. Every antique pull on the drawers and cabinets was unique. If all this belonged to Helen, she had come into money.

"Anybody home?" No answer. So, what had made the scraping sound? Moving to the bottom of a wide wooden staircase, she shouted up to the third floor. "Hello!"

Helen appeared with folded sheets in her hands. Dropping the laundry, she raced downstairs like a kid instead of a middle-aged lady with white hair like Tonya's.

"Tonya!" Helen flung her arms open.

She stepped into Helen's embrace, but that touch released a flood of terrible memories. That hospital room in Toronto. Waldock moaning and shriveling away from Tonya's life-siphoning touch. It had saved Loon Lake, but Helen had used her.

"Nice place. Did insurance pay for it?"

"You look good."

"I knew it! You charmed the insurance people, didn't you?"

"All that matters is we're alive, and you're finally free."

Tonya cleared her mind before she opened their telepathic link. *It's good to see you.* During Helen's visits to the cells under City Hall, bars had kept them apart and the Staff of Storms had prevented telepathy.

When did class get out?

"Hours ago." But Tonya didn't feel like explaining the detour to Kirkdene's farm.

Do you want me to beat up Marta for you?

It was their usual joke, since Marta was a high school bully, but when they laughed, it choked up Tonya. She had missed this. "How did you know she's in my class?"

"People talk. Have you made any new friends?" When Tonya shook her head, she pushed. "Try. You hate being alone." Helen gave Tonya a searching look. "What about your old friends?"

"Don't worry. I'm following the rules and staying away, but the minute my parole is over, I'll find Priya and introduce myself. I need my best friend back, even if she never remembers. And I can't live without Drake."

"Don't."

"We were in love."

"If you awaken his memories, Ashton Security will erase his mind again. Each spell reinjures the brain, and Donna would enjoy hurting him to punish you." Helen's cheeks were hollow, the lines on her face pronounced. The past few months had aged her.

"Someday"

"Never. The closer your relationship, the more danger of stirring Drake's memories."

"But after I've finished the magic course ..."

"Sorry. The Mundanes can never know."

Helen wouldn't lie about that, which meant the only way to get back Priya and Drake was to convince the City Council to hold another tribunal. How could she, a teen without magical training or connections, make them listen? It seemed impossible, but if there was a way, she had to find it.

12

Tonya was leaving when Donna Ashton led her elder brothers, Marvin and Stephen Jr., up the central aisle of the store with Tonya's parole officer and former jail guard, Miranda, trailing behind. They all wore Ashton Security gray, except for Donna in her black skirt suit and red blouse.

Tonya telepathically alerted Helen on the third floor. *The Ashtons are here. Shouldn't your wards have kept them out?*

What wards? Using magic would give them ammunition against me.

"Bring us Helen Lennox." Donna grinned, patting her back-combed mane with ruby-tipped fingers.

"Why?" Tonya stalled to let Helen escape.

"She's a wanted criminal by order of City Council."

"Why now?" The investigation concluded that Tonya had accidentally destroyed Waldock with her uncontrolled powers.

"We released you because Helen confessed to murdering Jack Waldock."

"She's innocent!" Tonya blurted.

"Is she?" Miranda stepped so close Tonya could see the jailor's freckles. "Be careful what you say. An eyewitness says you murdered Waldock together."

"No." Tonya kept her voice calm. "My friends vouched for her at the hearing." But that was before Ashton Security wiped their memories. "Helen settled a revenant, and that's not murder."

"According to what witness?" Donna asked.

The only one who hadn't suffered a memory wipe. "Roberto Alvarez."

"Helen tried to charm him." Donna smirked. "But he came to his senses, and now the good people of Loon Lake are going to come to theirs. It's time to sweep out the corruption and reform Loon Lake."

Tonya trembled, fists clenched at her sides. This wasn't about clearing out shady politicians. Her whole life, the truce between Pures and Trads had prevented Old Families from using magic. It protected the Mundanes and kept the Mods in check, which they hated. Before they took charge of security, the Ashton family had been poor and powerless, but not anymore. Tonya guessed they had enough clout to make the City Council prosecute Helen for using magic, no matter if it had saved Loon Lake.

Old Loon Lake had stamped out open magic use a hundred years prior. The long-standing tradition got reinforced in the 1990s when Jack Waldock and his pal, Len, intimidated citizens. If businesses and farms refused to pay their gang protection money, flames razed their assets. Loon Lakers knew the fires were arson, but the Mundane fire marshal couldn't find proof. Waldock's gang paid frightening visits to witnesses who suddenly refused to testify.

It was a terrible time, and a business opportunity. Stephen Ashton Sr. saw that Mundane law enforcement was powerless against magic. He offered private security to the Old Families who could scarcely refuse. Peaceful times returned, while the Ashtons grew fat off the council coffers. In his final years, Stephen Sr. scarcely left the family compound, but Donna and her brothers expanded the business and built jail cells under City Hall.

Junior Ashton puffed out a mountainous chest, his tiny head perched like a pebble. "Let's lock them both up."

Marvin deflated his brother with a look. As tall as Junior, he was slimmer and softer spoken. "Logically, you were guilty until Helen confessed. Either she coerced you into helping her murder Waldock."

"Or you did it together." Donna's smile reminded Tonya of Marta.

Helen came downstairs, her head held high. "Tonya did nothing."

"Council should strip their powers and banish them both." Marvin took up position beside Helen as he and Junior marched her to the front of the store where Donna and Miranda waited.

Tonya stood in their path until Miranda whispered, "Don't. If you resist, they can charge you, too."

"I have to do something."

"Breaking your parole won't help."

"Hands behind your back and turn around." Junior looked to Marvin.

"Good job, bro. Put on the handcuffs."

"You should be giving Helen a medal." Tonya wanted them to know she knew. "She saved our city even though Waldock was killing her with cancer."

"Sounds like a motive." Donna tapped on her phone.

What should I do? Tonya asked telepathically.

Helen's interior voice was calm. *Let them take me, then tell the witch's advocate. My spare keys are in the drawer under the cash register.*

But if they put you in a cell, Donna can use the Staff of Storms to steal your powers!

Helen's voice in Tonya's head sounded deadly calm. *Tell the witch's advocate to see Mayor Thornton. He opposed jailing you and wants to stop the Ashtons from controlling Loon Lake.*

13

Tonya drove Helen's dark green Honda Civic east along Lakeshore Drive to the strip of parkland across the southern end of the city. Past campus, the lake narrowed at the eastern end of town, allowing Tonya to see the far shore. Elizabeth Carke, witch's advocate, lived in a big waterfront house beside the park.

Leaving her car in the long driveway between houses, Tonya knocked at the side door, turning to appreciate the lake view while she waited. No answer. The last time she'd spoken to Carke had been at her trial. For Helen's sake, Tonya hoped the advocate would do better this time.

Tonya knocked louder. Twice.

Eventually, Carke answered the door, her blonde hair tucked under a paint-stained cap.

"Do you have a minute?"

"A quick one." Carke led Tonya inside, stooping to grab an empty liquor box on her way to the kitchen. She set it on the table. "What do you need?"

"Ashton Security arrested Helen."

"I warned her this would happen if she testified you were innocent."

"They're charging her with murder."

"Mayor Thornton will give both sides a fair hearing." Carke took a stack of dishes from the cupboard, wrapped one in newspaper, and set it into the box.

"There shouldn't be a hearing. Waldock was already dead when Helen forced him to materialize."

"She used death magic in a public hospital."

"How do you plan to defend her?"

"Folks are afraid of Helen, and the Mods are out for blood."

"She's not a murderer."

"Doesn't matter." Carke bundled another dish in newspaper.

"If we prove she didn't kill Waldock, they'd have to let her go, right?"

Carke put the dish in the box. "Public magic use is a misdemeanor, but Helen has enemies." She picked up a stack of pink plastic dishes and shoved them into the box.

It was clear the advocate was fleeing the fight. "Helen told me Betty could vouch for her. Who's Betty?"

"An extreme recluse. Lives on Grand Island. As teens, Helen says she had an affair with Waldock. They used to disappear for weeks. Poof, gone." She mimed exploding fingers.

"Magically?"

"The last time they went missing, Waldock wouldn't talk about it. He went back to hanging out with Len as if nothing happened."

"So?"

"Betty never left the island."

"They killed her?"

"No, she became a squatter." Carke opened a cabinet and grabbed dishes willy-nilly, layering them into a box with newsprint. "When Helen met him, they'd just broken up."

"Why would Betty stay on the island?"

Carke bit her knuckle, glancing sidelong at Tonya. "I don't know."

"Her testimony would have forced them to drop the charges."

"She won't talk to me." Carke edged away, but Tonya moved with her.

"Convince Mayor Thornton. He can sway City Council and get Helen released."

"Um, I think you should watch this." Carke pulled a phone out of her pocket and opened the Old Family phone app.

14

On the tiny screen, Donna's lips glistened and she faced the camera, patting her hair-sprayed mane in place. She glowed with health as she stood behind Mayor Thornton who slumped at his desk, his complexion ashen.

Donna dusted her crimson fingernails against her chest. "Good people of Loon Lake, the mayor thanks you for your generous support." Donna played to the camera, embracing viewers with a warm smile like their dear auntie. "And now, Mayor Thornton!"

To push himself upright, he braced his palms on his desk. A gray-haired man, Thornton wore a suit, silk tie, and pocket puff in different tones of gray. His campaign shtick was to see issues in shades of gray so he could represent Pures and Trads (symbolized by white), and Mods (symbolized by black). It was more optics than reality, because his Trad-friendly policies suppressed public magic use and punished those who used it. The mayor put on a show of supporting Mod magic use—if they kept it private.

Thorton blinked dull eyes at the camera.

Why was he moving so slowly?

"Many have asked about my health." He wheezed.

That was news to Tonya.

"Don't worry about me or Loon Lake. My former rival is an excellent leader able to heal our special city in these challenging times. Until I feel well enough to discharge my duties, I appoint Donna Ashton to act on my behalf." He collapsed into his chair.

Councilors leaped to their feet, some crowding close, others standing back. Their shocked expressions mirrored Tonya's thoughts. Why would Thornton endorse his bitterest rival?

Paramedics appeared so swiftly they might have been on standby. They bundled Thornton onto a stretcher and rushed him away.

Tonya searched Carke's face. "You knew about this?"

"The bad omens have been piling up. For sale signs, Mundanes moving out, Mods openly flouting the rules. I knew she'd make a move, but making the mayor sick? That's low, even for the Ashtons."

Thornton had been mayor since Tonya's childhood. Elected and re-elected, under Thornton, the Old Families knew the rules would never change.

Donna would bring a revolution.

Tonya shivered. The battle to suppress Donna's old ally, Waldock, had brought Tonya to the edge of death, and it had taken a month's bed rest to recover. In jail, Ashton Security guards denied her phone use and non-family visits for six months.

"We can't let them jail Helen, especially if Donna's in charge."

Carke's shoulders relaxed. "This isn't your fight. City Council will stop Donna eventually."

"I don't think so." The Mods controlled Thornton. Otherwise, why would a Trad mayor trust Donna whose family supported Waldock? Donna hadn't zombified the town directly, but Ashton Security was quick to memory-wipe the witnesses. On Halloween, Donna had tried to stop Tonya from preventing an outbreak. Inside their concrete compound, Donna's brothers used unauthorized magic. Midnight sightings of strange lights and sounds confirmed it.

"The Ashtons are too powerful. Anyone who stands up to Donna risks Marvin's financial wrath or Stephen Jr.'s physical threats."

"That's impossible to prove," Carke countered.

Tonya felt her cheeks heating. "Somebody has to stop these bullies."

Carke grabbed three mugs. "All you can do is appeal to the National Council and hope." She filled the box and folded the flaps closed. "Unfortunately, they usually agree with those in power."

"Donna is only the interim mayor."

"You watch. She'll get Council to approve a quick by-election and run for mayor unopposed. Who would risk a clash with the Ashtons?" Carke taped the box closed.

"And if Thornton feels better?"

"Exactly! Donna needs to become mayor in case he survives his coma."

"What?"

"I've seen Stephen Jr. use this spell before. Mayor Thornton is losing control of his body. Soon paralysis will start at his feet, climbing upward until his lips won't move."

"We have to stop him!"

"You can't. He talks like an eight-year-old, but Junior can drop you, no cure, no evidence."

A tiny wail interrupted them. Carke dashed out and, moments later, returned cuddling a newborn. Its wailing mouth dominated half its red face.

"Sorry, I have to feed the little guy. We're leaving in the morning." Cooing and rocking the baby in her arms, she waved Tonya to the door.

"Can't you stay until Helen's hearing? Show them there isn't enough evidence for a trial."

"You should leave, too. Helen's allies have targets on their backs, and I can't risk that anymore." Balancing the baby in the crook of her arm, she fished something out of her back pocket. "If you know anyone who wants a lakefront house, I'll give them a great deal for a fast closing date."

"Wait! How do I find Betty?"

"There's only one house on the island, but Betty won't talk. She sent a note through the lady who delivers her groceries. If I wanted to stay healthy, she warned me not to contact her again."

"Empty threat," said Tonya.

"Maybe." Carke walked Tonya onto the front step. "But Waldock had a taste for powerful girlfriends." She held the door with one hand, the other steadied the baby on her hip. "Who's to say what Betty can do if you make her angry? Goodbye."

"Have a safe trip." What Tonya wanted to say was don't sell the house. I'm going to make you safe and rip Loon Lake out of Donnas' grasping hands. But how could Tonya promise anything? She had no powers, no fighting skills, and no allies who remembered her.

When Tonya left Carke's house, the Paperboy of Christmas Past was waiting.

"How did it go?" the ghost kid asked.

"Must you follow me everywhere?"

"Like gum on a shoe. Your life is derailing, and I want the exclusive." He framed the headline in the sky. "Girl of Good Family Goes Down in Flames."

15

Driving to the pier, Tonya spotted a suspicious column of smoke. She accelerated until she could see Ted's Excellent Campground where flames engulfed a cluster of rustic cabins. Parking a safe distance away, she rushed past the fire to the lake, seeking a boathouse on the edge of Ted's property. There was a pump and hoses inside, if the flames had spared them.

Her heart pounded as she spotted the owner, soaking wet and covered in soot. Ted Kwok was a wiry old man who belonged to every service club and sang in three church choirs. As a kid, when the other kids had shunned Tonya, "Uncle Kwok" let her hang out in the camp office and eat penny candy.

A pump engine roared, one hose in the lake, the other in Ted's hand. He sprayed water onto the boathouse roof, soaking the surrounding grass, the lines in his tanned face pale against smudges of ash. "Grab the other hose!"

Tonya found a second hose in the boathouse and hooked it up to the pump. At Ted's direction, she aimed water at the nearest cottage.

"Caleb's store is gone, and mine's next unless we soak everything."

The camp office was gone too, and with it, Tonya's favorite picture of ten-year-old Ted hefting a pike as tall as he was. Behind him, Ted's unsmiling mother wore a blouse and skirt, black hair fastened in a bun. Ted's slender father carried a bait bucket and rested a hand on Ted's shoulder. His parents had immigrated from China in the fifties, and the campground was their legacy.

Campers congregated down by the beach, watching Ted and the volunteer firefighters spray the roof of the burning store. Tonya expected the looky-loos to start a bucket brigade, but they just stood there with empty hands, watching flames devour Loon Lake history.

16

THE SMOKE SMELL FADED as Tonya drove Helen's car toward the Ashtons' boathouse. Fires. It was always fires. They had started during her so-called Aunt Helen's teen years. Before last September, Tonya hadn't known Helen was her birth mother, but as a kid, she had lapped up any information about her exciting and powerful "aunt."

When her mom, Barbara, and Helen were kids, Mods were magic-trading bootleggers feared and admired for their outlaw glamor. Helen was a born catalyst who amplified the powers of others. She charmed animals and people so naturally that she hardly noticed breaking her Pure family's rules. Brenda, the woman Tonya grew up calling "Mom," criticized her sister's attitude. Now that Tonya had grown up and learned her parentage, Helen remained defiant.

Was it any surprise teenaged Helen had fallen for handsome Jack Waldock? The mayor's son rebelled against his wealthy family just as Helen rebelled against hers. Tonya had learned the story by reading between the lines, when her mother, Barbara, and "Aunt Helen" argued about the past.

Helen and Jack's romance blazed with a natural affinity for each other's magic. Jack delighted in channeling Helen's power into harmless magics like turning spring leaves red or making stale chips fresh. They found beauty in each new trick until Len came from the Mod side of the tracks to become Jack's best friend.

Influenced by Len, Jack tricked Helen into using her powers for necromancy. When she realized what he'd done, she dropped him as fast as it took for her hair to turn necro white. Not long after, Len and friends had Jack casting fireballs to destroy the barns and businesses of any Old Family who refused to pay protection money.

The Ashtons rose from outcast rebels to heroes when they became the City Council's best defense against a gang that incinerated its opponents. It surprised Helen later, when Len and the Ashtons conspired to raise Jack Waldock again. They hadn't liked him exactly, but Len's arson-loving ways had unwittingly led to their enormous success in the security business. Once the threat was gone, the need for security dropped off, and voters started complaining about the high taxes to pay for it.

When Tonya and Helen faced Waldock's revenant in the fall, their actions had prevented a new cycle of fiery intimidation. Or so Tonya thought, before Caleb's store burned. There would be no proof, but the Ashtons were responsible. Helen had caught them conspiring to grasp more leverage over Loon Lake.

The clubhouse for young Mods perched on the lakeshore close to the marina. At night, their music polluted the beach for miles, like a frat house for the Dark Arts. Nobody was brave enough to complain. On the weekends it was busy with a private beach, jet skis, race boats, plus the Ashtons' motor launch to speed partiers to Grand Island to cast spells in defiance of the law.

Sometimes Tonya envied her carefree Mod neighbors and their toys. As a Pure, Mom had tried to make her feel superior. Mostly, it made her feel alone. But not today. She planned to sneak in and search through Mod records and memorabilia. The Old Families were obsessed with their traditions and history. There had to be photos and accounts of the fatal Mod trip to the Island in 1995.

In Loon Lake, people didn't lock their doors during the day, and only a fool would try to steal from the Mods. On a weekday, it should be easy to slip into the clubhouse and take a look around.

The boathouse was a two-story building with an extensive terrace, firepit, and a long dock wide enough to accommodate a cluster of Muskoka chairs. Speedboats and inflatables bobbed on the water, tied up to the oversized dock. It was a reversal carried out within Tonya's short lifetime.

When she was little, Trad families pitied the Ashtons. They squatted on the worst land beside the local garbage dump. Forbidden to use magic, and excluded from "good" society, they scraped by on odd jobs. The kids wore hand-me-downs. The men wore jeans and ratty t-shirts, while Donna and Marta sported the latest styles from Walmart and The Salvation Army.

Everything had changed when Tonya was in grade six and Len recruited Jack Waldock. Before he went bad, Loon Lakers had never locked their doors. After, they installed security systems and smoke detectors on every floor. Frightened folks joined waiting lists to buy twenty-four-hour surveillance from Ashton Security. Those who did never saw a spark, while neighboring barns burned.

To go from unemployed, to hospital receptionist, to city councilor, Donna had completely transformed her look. Her professionally coiffed mane, three-inch heels, and her red and black power suits inspired awe and anxiety. For reasons obscured by lost records, the city deeded Councilor Donna's family the land they had been squatting on. And the dump? Every mound of garbage disappeared overnight like magic. During Tonya's teen years, the land surrounding the Ashton family compound grew private signs and fences to repel riffraff like Tonya.

She marched up to the wooden gate. A painted stencil depicted the Three-Century Ash, emblem of Old Family power. Some prankster had painted orange flames licking up the tree trunk. Tonya paused. She had burned down the Ash. This looked aimed at her personally.

The gate screeched open. "You must be lost." Marta stood with her arms across her chest.

"Is Arjun around?"

Marta scoffed.

"Guess I'll go then."

"I don't think so."

The sand gave way beneath her, swallowing Tonya to the thigh. Struggling sank her even faster.

"This is how we deal with spies." Marta shot Tonya the smirk that launched a thousand barbs.

"I'm quitting the Trads because I belong with the Mods."

"Is that right? In that case, come in." She flung open the door, smirking as Tonya continued to sink.

Marta had excluded Tonya from her clique in high school, but her boyfriend Shin had found Marta lovable. The Ashton adults were Helen's enemies, but Tonya had grown up with Marta. When she suffered during the campus epidemic, Tonya had even tried to help her. They'd never be friends, but they didn't have to be enemies.

Grabbing the bottom of the gate, Tonya hauled herself to the edge of the quicksand and pulled herself out onto her belly. Released, she stumbled to her feet between a beach volleyball court and racks stacked high with kayaks and paddle boards. Up ahead, Marta stopped behind the main boathouse.

With a deft hand gesture, Marta transformed the wooden a-frame into a stucco building. A striped awning grew out of the side, sheltering a stone patio with wrought-iron tables and chairs like a Mediterranean café.

Tonya tried not to gasp. "Nice."

Marta sat at the table, and Tonya sank into the chair opposite. On contact with the wrought iron, her view changed. Boat racks and sand faded into an ocean view, and seagulls flew silently overhead. Dazzling aqua water contrasted with climbing oleander. The illusion was so realistic, she could practically smell the blossoms.

"I love your view."

"Why should I listen to you?"

"I never chose to be a Pure or a Trad. It's not my fault City Council ordered me to study magic with the Mods."

"Think you're badass 'cause you've done jail time? It doesn't make you cool, just unbelievably sad." Marta made big puppy eyes at Tonya and pretended to cry. With a gesture, she caused snakes to emerge from the armrests and wind around Tonya's wrists and ankles, crushing them against the wrought iron.

Straining against her bonds, Tonya tried to rock the chair, but it wouldn't move. "We don't need to be enemies. Helen should have been a Mod. We were born into the wrong tradition."

Marta scowled.

"Do you think I enjoy being a Pure when the Mods could give me this?" Tonya gestured with her head at the Italian seaside.

Marta grinned, and her cheek twitched. It was her tell, and it sent a shiver down Tonya's back. She'd last seen that expression in high school, right before Marta's mean-girl friends flushed Tonya's purse in the toilet. She braced herself as the snakes around her arms raised their heads and hissed, ready to strike.

Marta pushed her face too close to Tonya's. "Switching sides is the smart move, which is why I don't trust you. Cast one spell, drain the tiniest bit of magic, and we'll know." She pointed at Tonya's ankle monitor.

"You're not my parole officer." The serpents coiled tighter, numbing her hands.

"I own Ashton Security."

"Your mom does."

"She trusts me because we're a proper family, something you wouldn't understand."

Hearing sounds from the boathouse, Tonya shouted. "Let me go! Help!"

Marta laughed.

Arjun hurried in her direction as Tonya tipped the chair back and forth, trying to escape her hissing bonds.

"Tonya? Are you okay?"

On the forward swing, the snakes binding her to the chair vanished and momentum dashed Tonya to the ground head first.

Arjun stood over her. "How do you fall out of a chair?"

"Ask Marta."

But Marta had fled along the side of the building. When Tonya stood, the Mediterranean illusion was gone. "That witch!" She left Arjun, raced around the boathouse, and hammered on the clubhouse door.

When her fists didn't make enough noise, she kicked the bottom of the door until the wood split.

Marta opened up suddenly and hauled Tonya in by the shoulder, sending her stumbling into the entryway. Marta slapped Tonya's face, then shoved her back out, and tried to slam the door on her. Before it could close, Tonya grabbed the knob.

Big mistake.

A shock jolted her rigid, her muscles all spasming at once. Tonya willed her hand open but couldn't control it. She saw stars and felt herself passing out as the magical power cut, tumbling her into blackness.

How long was she out for? They grabbed her arms, but she resisted. Pain lanced through her head. Five of them, maybe six, dragged her into a room where sunlight warmed her face through open windows and doors. Teens, a few from her graduating year, gathered around to look down at her.

"Are you okay?

It was hard to focus, but that voice sounded familiar. "Fine." She tried to sit, but her head spun, and she collapsed back on the hardwood. Above her, a fringe of wavy black hair framed a friendly face.

"Arjun?" She saw him clearly.

He helped her sit.

"How can you be with the Mods?"

"I'm a new pledge."

Half a year ago, the City Council wouldn't have allowed outsiders to learn Old Family secrets. In the Mod clubhouse, Arjun was running with an insular clan. If they accepted Arjun, who had grown up in Toronto, it proved Mod membership rules were changing and evolving—except when it came to her. The best she could do was get out quickly before Marta hazed her again.

Arjun helped Tonya to her feet in a large room lined with bookshelves. Sports pennants dangled from cork boards. Framed black and white photos lined the walls, depicting mustachioed cricket teams and women in bonnets. The beachwear photos were chronological, starting with men's one-piece bathing costumes and ladies' swim dresses from the 1800s. They progressed through neon pink suits and men's Speedos around the 1980s before coming up for air in the 2000s. The series concluded with a framed poster of team captains Marta and her boyfriend Shin, flanked by the Loon Lake diving team.

"Nice pic," said Tonya.

"Thanks." Marta avoided mentioning Tonya's disastrous diving tryout, which gave her the courage to push for more info.

"Not your poster." She pointed to a framed picture in which a teenaged Jack Waldock stood beside Len. A girl lurking behind them wore dark braids complimenting a round face like Marta's. It had to be Donna. Helen looked nearly Waldock's age, her hair still chestnut brown. Len looked brawny and tanned, nothing like the frail old man Tonya had met. In the background of every picture, a pair of young girls worshipped Jack with puppy dog eyes.

"If she's okay, she belongs outside," Marta commanded.

None of the Mods volunteered until Arjun said, "I'll take her."

When the door closed behind them, he lowered his voice. "What are you trying to do?"

"Join the Mods."

"Why, when Marta hates you?"

"I'm impressed you picked that up. She's very subtle."

Arjun laughed.

"You're the only person who remembers me and doesn't hate me."

Marta stuck her head out a window. "Still talking?"

Arjun shrugged at Tonya. "Go, before she loses her temper." He entered the clubhouse without a backward glance.

Inside the fence, she could snoop around the boats, but the watercraft looked new. The clues to Waldock's disappearance lay with Helen's generation. Visiting the Mods had failed. Time to try Betty. Either the recluse would offer to help clear Helen's name—or Tonya would have to force her.

The sun had dropped low in the sky. It made Tonya shiver to think what spiteful things Marta could have done if left alone with her unconscious body. Sweat beaded Tonya's forehead despite the evening breeze. Dust swirled from the gravel stuck to her face.

As she reached for the car door, ectoplasm chilled her shoulder blade. It was the annoying ghost boy gripping her.

"Buck up! Why so down in the mouth?"

As if she hadn't suffered enough already! Ignoring him, she flung open the car door and got in.

"Don't be glum, Miss. You have me. Oh, looky!" He kneeled to the ground and a furry black streak dashed at his open arms. "A kitten!" He tried to grab it, but the cat chased the movement of glowing arms as if they were laser pointers. He twirled his arm, giggling. "I've wanted a cat all my life."

"Ghosts can't keep pets. How are you going to feed it?"

His smile sputtered out like a candle, then flamed again "You can feed her for me, and we'll call her Spot."

Tonya slammed her door, hoping to be left alone, but he glided through the door into the passenger seat. "What are you scheming?" He tilted his head. "Burning more trees? Committing another murder?"

Enough! She left the car and strode off, the ghost tailing her and nattering about her crimes. Jogging outran the conversation.

Suddenly, he was in her path, too quick to avoid. She ran through him with a sensation like plunging through ice water.

She turned on him. "You could've given me a heart attack!"

"Dames are so dramatic! Be rational. Look at my side of things. I could stay a paperboy for life, or, if I play my cards right, you could give me the scoop of a lifetime. Then they'll have to make me a reporter."

"You look nine years old."

"Nine going on 75." His head dropped. "And still waiting for my lucky break."

"I'm leaving, and I won't be granting any interviews."

With dusk descending, the little phantom out-glowed the fireflies. Elbows poked out of his frayed coat and toe holes sprouted from his shoes. The sight tugged on her heart and would make her pity him, if he weren't so annoying.

"Go!"

He kicked at the dirt without raising dust. "Geez! I know when I'm not wanted. C'mon, Kitty!"

The kitten leaped out of the bushes and purred after him. Poor waif. To be a ghost, he must have unfinished earthly business, but she had to focus on Helen's problem.

17

PRIYA SET DOWN THE acetylene torch and tipped open her welding helmet. Through the studio's floor-to-ceiling windows, she watched boats silhouetted against dimly lit water. The June heat made her mouth dry as sweat trickled down her back. The strain of melding steel to steel strained her shoulders, building muscle in a good burn. She lifted off her helmet and guzzled from a water bottle, but it was too hot to remain inside.

Outside, she sat on a bench facing Loon River and let the breeze cool her face. Across the placid water, a Canada goose led her flotilla of fuzzy gray goslings. By fall they would be large enough to migrate south, the strongest leading the V-formation, with the oldest and youngest drafting behind for easier success.

What worked for geese should work for people. At home, Priya fit into the family flock—or used to. The youngest, and Papa's favorite, the family formation had felt less restrictive in childhood. As a teen, she had still strained to please him. Silly goose. You can't stay under your parents' wings forever. Today she would work up the courage to announce her intentions in an email.

Zain walked up as she dictated the last words into her phone. "Whatcha doing?"

He was sort of sweet, with his goofy smile and two cameras slung around his neck.

"Nothing." Priya's eyes dropped to her phone. Should she send the message?

Zain must have read indecision on her face because he grabbed for the phone. Priya retreated, holding it behind her back. He leaped forward and the momentum swung a heavy camera into her other arm.

"Ouch!"

"Sorry, are you okay?" Zain frowned. He lifted her arm by the wrist. "I don't see a bruise." Reaching under her arm, he grabbed the phone and danced away. "Email." He punched the air. "I bet it's juicy!" He zigzagged out of her reach as he read out loud:

"Dear Papa and Ma,

I'm rocking a studio course in arc welding. Imagine me, your little daughter, building a sculpture as tall as a tree. I know welding isn't the most obvious path for an artist ..."

Zain grinned. "But just think. Until I'm famous, I can work at a shipyard!"

"I did not say that!" Priya lunged for the phone.

Zain sprang away. "What's the big deal? It's not even X-rated." He cleared his throat daintily and put on an upper crust British accent to read the rest:

"Does the family really need another doctor or engineer? I'm a born artist. Forgive me, at least until I get famous enough to make you proud.

Love,

Priya"

"Don't apologize." He waved the phone at her sculpture. "They'll go nuts when they see this sexy beast. I'm gonna send a pic."

"Stop!"

Zain held the phone over his head, forcing Priya to jump for it.

"Too late. I got it." Zain laughed. "Let's wow Papa." He poised his finger to tap send. "Ready?"

Out of nowhere, Drake snatched it away.

"Hey!" Zain gave Drake a shove. "We're just having fun. Priya, tell him."

Drake handed Priya the phone. "You okay?"

"Yeah. Time to get back to work."

"Good news first," said Drake. "Meet Grace, our new star."

The girls smiled and waved hello.

"So, we're really doing this?" asked Priya.

"Yeah, so quit with the dinosaur and give us our monster," said Zain.

"Patience." Priya cracked her knuckles. "Bring the Ninjas back tomorrow, and I'll show the whole crew."

"Good deal," said Zain.

"And?" Drake nudged Zain.

Zain pushed him back.

"Don't you want to say something to Priya?"

"Have a nice solder?"

"You could apologize."

"For what?"

"Do you even understand consent?" Drake rolled his eyes.

"That applies to texting her dad?"

The way Zain tilted his head made Priya laugh.

"I was trying to help. I mean, look at this." Zain pointed at the half-finished armature. "When her family sees it, they are going to freak out!"

"Yup." Priya slipped on her helmet.

It was a relief when they filed out and let her work. Most of her projects began with elaborate plans which emerged over months. This piece refused to conform to diagrams as instinct controlled her hands in an artistic flow. Soldering came easily, her execution better each day. Could such control come from mere practice?

She thrummed with inspiration as if unseen powers directed her hands to give birth to a living beast.

Late that night, Priya thought she saw movement outside the studio. Could her monster be stirring? Preposterous. Still, she shivered and searched the darkened lake and sky, unwilling to look directly at the beast she was building.

The rumble of a motorcycle roared beside the studio. Priya rushed to the door, but by the time she reached the road, all she saw were receding taillights.

18

To speak to Betty, Tonya needed a boat. Facing the water, the marina office was white with aqua blue trim, topped by a flat roof that served as a patio. Walking from the parking lot to the beach, she spied Shin on the sand between the office and the docks, applying sealant to a cedar strip canoe. His black hair had escaped his white bandana, and resin splattered his ripped denim shorts. His muscles flexed smoothly with each brushstroke, but she was only interested in Drake.

"Staring at a half-naked man." The newsboy ghost trailed behind her. "Shameless!"

She rushed to get by Shin before he noticed her.

"Tonya!"

Too late.

"Wait, how are you?" Shin stood, paintbrush in hand. "I heard you were really sick."

"I'm better now." As far as Mundanes knew, she'd been in a Toronto hospital, not a prison cell.

As he took a better look, Shin's mouth opened in a wolfish smile. Typical male. When she'd been overweight, he'd never looked at her.

"You look great."

"Yup, but still not ready for the diving team." He could stop staring any time.

"Diving isn't everything."

"Just the only thing," Tonya quoted his girlfriend's tagline. "How is Marta?" If Shin didn't remember Halloween, he would have forgotten dropping Marta for Priya.

"I think you know the guy she's dating now."

"Who?"

"Brown guy, operates a camera for the Digital Ninjas?"

"Arjun?" That was fast, and awful, but Marta's face was stunning, and her body smoking hot. Over the years, Tonya had watched her looks blind many guys to her nature. "Sorry for your loss, I guess?"

"It's okay. I'm happy for her."

"That's big of you." Maybe he wasn't such a jerk. He had dated Priya after all, and she loved to put a chauvinist in his place.

He gestured back at the canoe. "I have to work, but we should get together sometime."

"That would be great."

She hoped he meant it, and not on account of his swimmer's shoulders. Shin was nervy and sometimes treated girls like trophies, but Priya had brought out his sensitive side. In the amnesia-scarred clusterduck her life had become, Tonya decided to give him a chance. She desperately needed a friend.

Comfortable in anything from a power boat to a kayak, Tonya intended to rent a cheap aluminum outboard until sunlight glinted on a turquoise Sea-Doo in the rental office window. She fell in love. Sleek. Beautiful. Fast. Why not enjoy the ride? She dashed inside, flashed her boating license, and signed the rental agreement.

By the time she emerged from the office, Shin had rolled the Sea-Doo's trailer to the boat slip beside the dock. Light danced on its flecked metallic finish.

Shin pushed the PWC into the water and waded in, positioning it beside Tonya on the dock. "The owner just bought this. Don't scratch the paint."

"Don't fret." She threw a leg over and sat as Shin pushed her offshore. Tethered to her life jacket, she worked the key, turned the throttle, and roared out of the marina, expelling a rooster tail of spray. Tonya let the wind whip her hair as she curved left then right, leaning into the turns. Once she had a feel for the steering, Tonya opened the throttle and headed for Grand Island.

Soaked but smiling before she got halfway across the lake, Tonya decelerated, squinting at the passing shoreline for signs of life. Loon Lake got choppy near the island. The waves were lifting and dropping her PWC when she saw cedar trees on the rocky shore. She dropped her speed and orbited the island, looking for signs of habitation.

Trolling, Tonya passed mossy cabins with caved-in roofs. The coast was rocky, with conifers growing up to the shore blocking her view of the interior. Great. She would have to slog through heavy underbrush.

Had she passed something glittering between the trees? She slowed, doubled back, and spotted a tiny natural beach sheltered in a stand of pine trees. Slowing to a crawl, she aimed for shore, cut the engine, and let herself drift.

When momentum brought her close enough, Tonya hopped into the shallows and tugged the Sea-Doo onto a patch of golden sand. Dragging it past the waterline, she tied up to a gnarled pine so the wind couldn't carry away the shiny new craft.

Out of the waterproof compartment, she grabbed running shoes and binoculars. Her life vest, with the ignition key on a tether, stayed with the Sea-Doo. Next, she finger-combed her hair to meet the reclusive witch. As if her appearance was the most important factor. Triggering magic traps should concern her more, especially with that pesky newspaper ghost buzzing around her like a gnat.

Or was he? After dogging her from the marina to the middle of the lake, he had disappeared.

"Off my property!"

A lady almost Tonya's height marched into view. She had trimmed her gray hair into a helmet shape. Her left arm swung military style while the other held a rifle snug against her shoulder.

Tonya put up her hands. "Betty?"

"Get on your noisy sea flea and don't come back."

"Please. I need your help to save a woman's life."

"I'd rather shoot your foot off. Don't try your mind tricks on me!"

"I can't use magic." Tonya lifted her pant cuff. "This anklet makes sure of it."

"Liar. You're always sneaking around, charming this and warding that." Bracing her legs, the woman took the rifle off her shoulder and lowered it at Tonya.

"Wait! I'm not Helen."

"Guilty conscience, white hair, arrogant attitude, always wants something. If it quacks like a duck," she pointed the barrel at Tonya's chest and aimed through the gunsight, "it should die like one."

"I'm Tonya! Helen is my birth mother."

"Oh?" With one hand, the woman set the rifle butt in the sand. With the other, she patted down her shirt pockets and slipped on a pair of glasses. "You're not innocent."

"Yes, I am."

"Not with necro hair."

"My hair turned white helping Helen save Loon Lake from Jack Waldock. Or don't you get the news here?"

"Killing you will be the perfect revenge." She picked up the rifle again.

"Wait! I'm here to find out how Jack died."

"Is that right?" She aimed the gun at Tonya.

"Helen's in jail for killing him, but we returned an undead thing to rest."

"Hmph." Shouldering the rifle like a soldier, the woman quarter turned and marched away.

"Wait!" Tonya hurried after her. "You knew Jack and Helen as teens. Helen said you witnessed his death."

"Helen lies," Betty called over her shoulder without pausing in her climb up a treed hill.

"Donna wants her executed."

Tonya stumbled after Betty, who skipped rock-to-rock like a goat. Halfway up the hill, Tonya spotted a massive cottage with gables and a wrap-around porch. It should have been visible from the beach below but wasn't. Everything about it felt unreal, from the steep stone path to the cedar shake siding, which shone in the green forest light.

With closed eyes, Tonya opened herself to ambient energy. She saw through the illusion revealing a wooden staircase. It was easy to sprint after Betty now, but her mind, once opened to the life force surrounding her, demanded more.

Greedily, it sought deep reservoirs of energy in the trees and animals of the island until pain struck her head and she stumbled. Her temples throbbed and her vision blurred. Had the crone attacked her with magic?

No, worse. The prison anklet sent a throbbing pain through her leg strong enough to trip her up. Miranda had warned her with glee that she would suffer if she manipulated life force. How unfair! She hadn't tried to use magic when she gazed through Betty's illusion. Was it her fault her ability sought conduits of magic to supply her with magical life force?

Taking a deep breath, Tonya doubled her run up the stairs, but Betty slammed the door and threw the bolt.

Hearing that, Tonya needed a better strategy. Betty's testimony was Helen's best chance for freedom, but how could she convince Helen's enemy to defend her?

Crossing the deck, Tonya knocked on the door. "Betty, please, I just want to talk."

Every blind rolled closed simultaneously. Great. Tonya had messed up everything, and now Betty wouldn't testify. Carke warned her this would happen.

Without Betty's testimony, the only way Tonya could free Helen was to find out who killed Jack Waldock herself. That would wipe the smirk off Donna's face. The Ashtons were hiding something. Betty's fear convinced Tonya that the Ashtons were threatening the witness, but she needed proof.

When Tonya worked in her shop, Helen had delighted in teaching her forbidden knowledge. Despite her Pure family heritage, Tonya had learned that necromancy left trace residues which faded with time. With innate magic-sensing abilities, Tonya might pick up something if dark powers had been used nearby.

Grand Island was covered in pines and cedars with a rocky dome at the west end of the island. From Betty's balcony, the terrain resembled a leafy green dragon, curled around an enormous egg.

As a kid, Tonya remembered begging her father to land their boat on the shore, so she could see if the egg was real. "No, this is Mod territory," Mom had insisted. It was her rule to ban Tonya from mixing with magic users.

Tonya had obeyed until the spring she turned sixteen and cut class with a handful of classmates. They had piled into a fishing boat and tied up at the island's pier. It was fun swimming on the beach there. Later, they wandered through the forest, Tonya eager to find traces of clandestine magic. Lured back to the beach by a bonfire, Tonya never did find traces of magic, but she'd never reached high ground. Maybe that was where the Mods cast secret spells.

There was a cave entrance atop the central mound, which Tonya had always avoided. Scared of heights, she never saw the point in climbing a slippery granite hill just to drop through a narrow shaft into darkness.

But a hard-to-reach cave would be the perfect place to cast forbidden spells—or kill someone. Sweat dripped between her shoulder blades, and her arms itched with mosquito bites.

Was it foolish to climb up sheer rock in search of clues from before she was born? Betty was the last person to see Jack Waldock alive, and her willingness to pull a gun on Tonya raised suspicions. Carke said Betty had been there, the night of the crime, but even if Betty had murdered Waldock, it wouldn't save Helen if Tonya couldn't prove it.

Donna hated Helen and could coerce witnesses to manufacture a case. Influenced by Donna, the City Council wasn't even looking at the right crime. October's struggle in Helen's hospital room wasn't murder. To settle a revenant, Helen and Tonya had acted in self-defense.

Roberto had attacked them under Waldock's control that night. His undead ally, the pearl-wearing doctor, had disappeared from the hospital, but her existence proved that if Donna needed witnesses, she could dig one up. There was no guessing who else might fall under Donna's influence, and no way to exonerate Helen by proving reasonable doubt.

Mundane law worked that way, but the rival clans of Loon Lake thirsted to punish a criminal, and Donna would give them one.

With the odds stacked against Helen, Tonya had to overcome her fear of heights and turn over every rock until she found the real murderer. Pushing branches out of her face, it took an hour to reach the base of the stone egg. Up close, the hill glittered with pink and gray granite crystals. If Dad were there, he would pelt Tonya with facts about minerals, lakes, and receding glaciers, but she was alone. No safety net. No helmet. What made her think she could reach the summit?

She took a deep breath. Cool, spicy pine scents filled her lungs. Waves lapped the shore. Nature was her happy place, and the sounds and smells calmed her as she searched for the best way up. On the smooth surface, her shoes slipped, and she couldn't get a grip. It would take a helicopter to climb it.

All those years ago, she and her teenaged friends had searched the island without finding signs of death magic. The traces might have faded or been erased. Why risk a fatal fall looking for traces of a twenty-year-old crime that probably never happened? It seemed ludicrous—until she pictured Helen in a cell with all her hopes placed on Tonya.

Light peeked through the trees, drawing her away like a sign. Tonya followed the light into a clearing surrounded by a ring of trees. Pretty. A tidy meadow of buttercups and red Devil's paintbrush clung to one end of the granite hill. A ray of light full of glittering dust motes fell on a set of rusty footholds on the rock like rungs of a ladder.

Curiosity overcoming her fear of heights, Tonya climbed halfway to the top before she glanced down.

Oops.

The world started spinning. She gripped the rung above and held still to make the dizziness go away. *Don't look down. Don't close your eyes. Look at the pink, black, and white grains of granite in front of your nose.* Eventually, she forced herself to test the next handhold and take the next step. *Keep moving. Don't think. Ignore the head spins.*

Fists gripping the metal rungs so tightly they hurt, she willed herself to relax. The wind, which had felt exhilarating as she rode her Sea-Doo, snickered and whispered batting tendrils of white hair into her face. Protruding from the blistering rock surface, the iron spikes turned her fingers sweaty slick. Tonya exhaled through her nose as if this were a yoga class, not an attack of dizziness fifty feet above the ground. Falling would kill her, so she distracted herself with the sound of chickadee trills in the wind-stirred cedars and waited for her head to clear.

Once she could open her eyes, Tonya put one foot above the other and shifted one hand at a time. Yesterday, this climb would have been impossible.

But she had to save Helen.

19

The Hub Pub buzzed with late afternoon chatter. Priya sat in a booth, massaging her right shoulder, sore from welding.

"You started before me." Arjun fake-pouted.

"You'd better catch up, 'cause I'm drinking alone." Priya toasted him with ginger ale. It was their private joke since neither of them drank.

Arjun slid onto the bench facing her. "How are your parents?"

"Sweet, loving." She massaged her temples. "And oh so attentive."

"Driving you crazy, then?"

"As per usual. How can you handle having doctors for brothers?" She sipped her drink. "The parental pressure would make my head explode."

"Easy. I don't care." He tossed his hair ostentatiously.

"Liar."

"My parents worked hard for my tuition," his face lit up, "but their servants will have servants when I conquer Hollywood."

"Good luck with that. You sound like Zain."

"Unlike you, Miss Arty Farty, I'm operating a Steadicam when I graduate. They won't pay me in compliments."

"Why does nobody believe I can make it as an artist?"

"Sorry, do I sound like your parents?"

"No, like my big brother. Let me buy you a slice of cake."

"Sorry, Sis. Can't stay."

"What? I thought we had a date." It was her turn to fake pout.

"Forgive me? I have a real date. Do you know Marta?"

"Go for it, bro, but don't ask me to patch up your broken heart."

After he left, Priya debated whether to stay and eat alone.

"Is this seat taken?"

Priya locked eyes with a modern Adonis. "Uh."

His high cheekbones hinted at Andean origins, and his powerful torso begged to be sculpted. For a fleeting moment that thought tugged at something in her memory, and then it was gone.

"I'm Roberto. My parents just bought the Village Bakery."

"How nice for you."

"Was that guy giving you a problem?"

"No."

"He left in a hurry."

"I don't need rescuing."

"The independent type. Cool." He pulled a motorcycle helmet out of his bag. "See you around."

"Wait. Stay and eat with me?"

"Here?"

His surprise made Priya laugh. "Unless you want to take me for a ride?"

"I could spare some time."

Priya couldn't figure it out. A guy this handsome would be hard to forget, but he looked vaguely familiar. "Have we met?"

"I finished school last year."

When he batted his long eyelashes, it unleashed butterflies in her stomach. She burned to know the origin of his cute accent, but asking wasn't polite.

"We must have crossed paths on campus. I'm taking feminist studies." It was her best line for filtering out jerks.

"Not fine art?"

"You've been spying on me!"

"I run on the trail past the art studio every morning, and I love a woman who plays with fire."

"And this was going so well." She shook her head in mock sorrow.

"What are you making?"

Blood rose to her cheeks. It shouldn't matter if he liked her art, but it did. "What do you think?"

"Unique. Stunning."

Priya let out the breath she'd been holding.

"The sculpture's not bad, either."

She swatted at him. "You don't care about art! You have a thing for arc welders."

"It's a common kink." Roberto's chuckle faded. "What you tease out of steel thrills me."

When their eyes locked, she felt a tingle. Suddenly, the bench felt too hard, the café too loud. Her legs needed to move. "Can we go somewhere and talk?"

"Where?"

"Anywhere but here."

He zipped up his leather jacket. "Hungry?"

Sudden pangs made her nod.

"Good. Let's go for a ride."

Arms around Roberto's waist, hair escaping her helmet and thrashing in the breeze, Priya inhaled his leather and musk. First meeting, first date. If only her cousins could see her. They had teased her about going to a hick university instead of engineering school, or Ontario College of Art and Design.

She had left Toronto to escape her childhood bedroom, meet strangers, and have adventures. Her mother would faint if she saw her good little girl on a motorbike. Papa would have grounded her like a child.

The engine roared, and she leaned into every curve, willing the bike to go faster. So why was Roberto pulling in at the Condor Bakery? So much for born to be wild.

When they stopped, she whispered in Roberto's ear, "Can't we keep going?"

"I want you to meet my mother." He got off first and helped her off the bike.

Priya pulled off the helmet and shook out her hair. "Can't it wait till we're going steady?"

"I don't like waiting." His hand warmly embraced hers as he led the way.

It was her first visit to the Condor Bakery. A bell jangled overhead as they stepped inside, and she inhaled caramel and butter. A handful of iron tables filled the space in front of a wall-to-wall pastry case.

Roberto held a chair out for her.

Deliberately, Priya chose the opposite chair. Start as you mean to carry on. It was one of her father's better mottos.

"Ah, feminist studies." He sat opposite her.

On one wall, Andean women in distinctive fedoras lead llamas festooned with colorful yarn decorations. Three condors spiraled in the updraft above their terraced fields.

"Nice place."

"We just finished redecorating." He held up spattered fingers. "I'm still scrubbing the paint off my hands."

"You're an artist, too." That explained his interest.

"No, I paint with a roller. Madre works the magic."

A cheap guy would have chosen the family restaurant to save cash. Roberto's fancy bike killed that theory, so either he was crazy or controlled by his family. Was it wrong to wish for crazy?

"Your mother's talented." And cheesy, but who was she to judge? Maybe this expressed her taste, or maybe it matched local expectations for an ethnic restaurant. Hadn't this place been Scottish in the fall? She looked at the plaid upholstery on the café chairs and found confirmation. All summer she'd been forgetting things and having déjà vu.

A small woman with her hair in a black bun wearing a crocheted shawl appeared table side. Priya hadn't heard or seen her coming.

"What can I get you?"

"Hi, are you Roberto's mother?"

She nodded.

"Pleased to meet you. I'm Priya." She reached out to shake hands, but the woman pursed her lips.

Roberto's mother didn't reply but waited silently until Priya ordered tea.

"She'll have one of your special cakes," Roberto said. "Everybody loves them."

"I don't eat meat or eggs."

"I have perfect thing." The lady retreated noiselessly.

"There's egg in most pastries. What can she give me?"

"No clue, but avoid the empanadas. They're full of chicken." Roberto reached to take her hands.

Without thought, Priya flinched away, folding her hands in her lap. Instinct warned her to leave, but the tiny voice couldn't overcome her powerful curiosity. "Your family moved to Loon Lake?"

"After I graduated."

"Why not sooner?"

"Mami only discovered Loon Lake last year. Until she sent me to study here, she barely knew where Canada was."

Roberto's mother set a teapot between them. It was white bone china decorated with purple thistles. A thick plaid border decorated the cups and saucers. Priya vaguely remembered coming here and refusing Cornish pasties. A friend had brought her, a good friend, but who? Before she could tease out the memory, round cookies powdered with sugar appeared on the table.

"Try the alfajores." Roberto offered the plate. "They're our specialty."

Cookies had eggs in them. "They look lovely, but no thanks."

Roberto didn't put the plate down right away. The crumpled look on his face surprised her. What was the big deal about a little cookie?

His mother hovered as if waiting to see if she would try one.

"Sorry. I don't eat egg."

After Roberto's mother stalked away, Priya felt like she had failed a test. Time to end this. She scalded her lips chugging down the tea. Robert tried to refill her cup.

"No, thanks. Let's go."

Hurt-puppy eyes looked wrong on such a big guy. "You should feel honored to meet the family."

"I do, but I want to leave."

"One more cup first. You don't want to offend Mami."

Priya accepted the refill, and Roberto peppered her with questions. She told him about school, homework, the weather, but the whole time, Priya felt eyes drilling into her back.

Her heart raced, and she craved fresh air. Priya stood, half-empty cup abandoned on the table.

Madre materialized beside Priya, making her jump.

"One last little treat for such a pretty girl." The lady handed Priya a large sweet wrapped in waxed paper.

"No eggs?"

"No eggs. Only milk, nuts, sugar."

"Thank you." Priya unwrapped a log of homemade fudge and popped it in her mouth.

Roberto held the door. "Where to now?"

The confection expanded, flooding her mouth with syrup and preventing speech. She stumbled to his motorcycle and put on the spare helmet, still mute as they climbed aboard.

As they roared away, the sky spun sideways, then righted itself, leaving her dizzy. It must have been an optical illusion or mind trick. And it absolutely, probably, hopefully wasn't because the tea was psychedelic.

And the queasy twist in her stomach might have been caused by the motorcycle tilting into the turns, but she suspected it was the syrupy goo rolling down her throat and expanding in her guts like a greasy hand.

20

Roberto felt Priya's arms loosen around his waist as he leaned into the south turn and headed for the water. Behind the art studio, he braked gently so she wouldn't fall off the bike. He dismounted first and held out his hand.

She stumbled and fell into him. "Sorry." Her voice sounded thick, and she yawned.

"Am I boring you?" His tone teased and tested her alertness.

"No."

Her first yawn started a cascade of yawns he could only stop by taking Priya around the waist and looking into her eyes. "Stay awake. I promise this won't be dull." He smiled and walked her to the water. "See where the lizard's tail drags between its feet?" He pointed to tiny footprints in the mud which circled little mounds like melting sandcastles.

"You drove me here to see lizards?"

"Fire salamanders." He stood close, enjoying Priya's clean gingerbread and vanilla scent.

"These hands bring your sculpture to life." Moving behind her, he took her by the wrists and spread her arms wide in flight. "I will be your Zen master, teaching you the way of art."

"You have the worst pickup lines!" Priya giggled.

"Close your eyes. Picture every scale on its back and each claw on its feet."

"You're serious?" She twisted around to look up at him, her eyes lingering on his lips.

Roberto felt a pang of guilt. "Concentrate." This wasn't supposed to be a seduction. Energy crackled in the air, and white lightning arced from the water to Roberto's feet, sparking up his torso, and through his arms into her.

"What the?!" She let go, breaking the connection in a shower of sparks.

"Ow!" He glowered. "Next time, tell me before you let go."

She looked past his shoulder, eyes wide. "I can see every tip of every pine needle in the dark." Taking his hand, she dragged him to the shoreline. "Look, the stars aren't white.

They're twinkling pink, green, and blue." She turned on him. "Your face is glowing. What did you do to me?"

"Let me help you do more."

"You drugged me!"

"Not exactly. Do you feel sleepy?"

She backed away. "Leave me alone."

"If you wish, but we are tapping into enormous power. Don't you want to know everything it can do?"

"No."

But Roberto recognized the look on her face and knew she was lying. Back when he dated Tonya's roommate, Priya and Tonya had been inseparable. He'd had months to notice how much Priya loved learning about everything. Once he tickled her curiosity, she'd follow him anywhere.

Priya swayed, on the point of leaving, when she suddenly turned around and shoved him.

"I probably deserve that." And much more, but this was Madre's plan, and he had to obey. "Let's make the greatest dragon in the history of art!"

She laughed.

He didn't.

"I can make art by myself."

"Let me be your catalyst."

"Sounds like a fancy word for spiking my drink." She shoved him again, slipped, and accepted his hand to steady herself.

"A catalyst makes another person's magic stronger. Concentrate on your dragon." He moved behind her.

At first, she pulled away, but eventually, she leaned into him.

He took her hands by the wrists and held them up. "Close your eyes and tell me what you see."

"My dragon flies along the river, skimming the waves."

Roberto watched white fire arc from the top of Priya's head and into the sky over the river.

Suddenly, Priya ducked, as if an invisible beast were attacking.

Keeping hold of her hands, Roberto turned Priya to face him. "Why so scared?"

"The dragon roared." She tilted her head, craning her neck and looking into the starry sky. "Are you sure it won't eat us?"

Roberto snatched his hands back with a flash and a thunder crack.

"That stung! Why'd you let go?"

He tried to sound casual. "You've had enough for one night."

Her dark eyes pierced him. "Teach me how to control the magic."

"What magic? This was a visualization exercise to help you concentrate."

"Liar. At first, it seemed like a hallucination, but that shock was real. What did you do to me!"

"Nothing."

She glared up at him, vibrating with fury like a homicidal mouse. He chuckled.

"Turd for brains." Priya walked away.

"I'll make it up to you." Roberto rushed to catch up. "Let me drive you home?"

"Never mind. I'll crash here." She marched into the studio and slammed the door in his face.

21

AFTER MAKING SURE ROBERTO had left, Priya suited up for welding. Her research had started with birds until she remembered the flying fox. The largest bat in India, its wingspan stretched four feet but folded tightly around its eight-inch body for sleep. Priya smiled. If her creature were real, it would be the first dragon to eat mangoes and nap hanging upside down.

Buzzing with energy, she climbed the ladder to tackle the challenging join between the wings. As she applied metal plates to the wire armature, she wondered where a giant fruit bat would find jumbo bananas.

European dragons carried off cows and fairy princesses, but what about Canadian winter? Would her dragon swoop down on snowmobiles and snatch up skiers?

I would swim and catch fish.

Where did that thought come from? Was she dreaming? The weight of her helmet and the heat of the blowtorch in her glove proved she was awake. She shrugged it off. Anybody could hallucinate from fatigue and getting zapped with magic. Plus, auditory hallucinations hardly counted.

To stave off unwanted voices, Priya hummed a tune that rose and fell with waves on the beach. In a state of flow, she cut, placed, and soldered. Lifting plates and bars of metal should have been exhausting, but excitement drove her. Each new join brought her creation closer to life.

Who could sleep?

This pure inspiration had absolutely nothing to do with the thread of light running from the lake, up the ladder, and through her gloves.

Fever dreams. That's all it was. Light didn't flow like plasma, using people as its conduit. In the morning, she would wake in the dorm and forget these tea visions. Either that, or she was working magic and never wanted to stop. This sculpture was her best work, and she might never feel so inspired again.

Priya hardly noticed when the dark sky turned cloudy and hid the stars. Rain plopped against the studio windows, increasing until drops pelted the glass driven by tree-whipping winds. There was no lightning, if you didn't include the jagged lines of plasma joining the lake to her and her creature.

Thunder crashed. Rain battered the roof. It was a night to feel safe and dry inside while campers shivered in their tents. Falling trees took out the power lines, but Priya worked on by blowtorch and inspiration.

Through the studio windows, it was so dark that Priya failed to see Roberto in a boat offshore, observing her through binoculars.

22

THE APEX OF THE granite egg was a solar oven, burning Tonya's hands and knees. Sitting calmed the spinning world and slowed the blood rushing in her ears. She had done it!

Gingerly standing, she wiped her palms on her sweatpants. Without looking down directly, she spied three little bays on the shore protected by points of land. Betty's cove was too small and tree-covered to see, but Tonya spotted the pier where Betty received her groceries.

Would the prison anklet block her abilities this high from the ground? Eyes closed, she reached out to draw from the life force surrounding her.

Pain sliced at her temple, and the bracelet scorched her ankle, but not before she sensed something dark just out of reach. Eyes closed, she let the world recede into a matrix of pulsing lights, each one a living energy source. Trees, animals, birds, fish, and even algae balls suspended in the lake glowed with life.

Below the granite dome, she sensed an energy void. Where were the bats? The insects? A cave should support life, but something had blighted the cavern beneath this hill.

Fighting through the pain, she extended her mind further.

Weird. In the hollow under the mountain, darkness gathered like a roiling cloud, but it felt nothing like Helen's death magic. Something unnatural gathered in the space below, but what did it mean? Her gut told her to flee, but she had to know.

Farther afield, on the hillside where Betty lived, a cold and dark agony emerged from the earth, filling her head.

Thunder clouds darkened the sky, although sunset was a couple of hours away. In a meditative state, she felt nature press in on every side. Birds, squirrels, and insects filled the trees surrounding the granite egg. A hundred unique energy points tugged at her, begging her to siphon off just a little of that power. Her greedy mind had learned how to do so in crisis, but if Tonya gave in to that desire today, untrained and unsupervised, there was no telling if she could stop.

It took effort to close off that part of her mind. Taking power was forbidden, but sensing power might lead to a clue. She had to risk opening her senses a little.

There it was again.

Below the cheerful chirping of birds and scurrying of squirrels lurked another force, deeply buried and sinister. It didn't feel like life force or the ancestral magic she had felt in the catacombs.

A cold energy enveloped this island, and something massive lurked in the cave beneath her, but it was difficult to gage its form. Energy glowed from living things, too. They were large. People?

Mentally, she reached out to identify these glowing points of life, when, on a distant hill, she detected the traces of something terrible. Not since Jack Waldock's death magic coursed into her veins had Tonya felt this tar and sand sensation grating at her insides. There was no doubt.

Racing against sunset, she got down on hands and knees and reached back with one foot, feeling for the first iron rung. Climbing from a height would always test her, but she felt energized with certainty. Death magic had been cast near Betty's shack.

Now to prove Waldock was murdered and uncover the killer.

23

Through the rain-splattered studio window, lightning forked over the water, striking the island. Rain drove into the lake in rhythmic patterns accompanied by crashes of thunder. A sense of triumph welled inside Priya, thrilling up and down her spine. At last, she had done it.

The creature's body stood tall. To make it more real, she lay her palm against its chest. Heat-treated to a rainbow sheen, the scales reflected multicolored light with each flash of lightning. If only her parents could see her now.

Mother expressed her artistic talents through cooking and sewing. Her art was pure love but private. A hundred years from now, nobody would care about the color of pomegranate seeds floating atop her eggless custard. The family could love her mother's hand-embroidered clothes only until they wore out.

But Priya's sculpture would endure. Larger than any artwork in Loon Lake, Priya had seldom seen its equal. The closest was a giant spider sculpture she saw in Ottawa, but compared to that rigid beast, her creature vibrated with life.

A heartbeat thudded beneath her hand as she skimmed over its tough surface, marveling at how warm and dry it felt under her fingertips.

"Are you... alive?" she whispered.

In response, the beast shook its head like a dog shedding water, then brought its face down to hers, tilting its head and staring at her with eyes like red coals.

She backed away slowly.

The studio was the size of a hockey rink. If she ran for the door, it could pounce. She took another step back, holding its gaze. Then another.

A low growl shook the rafters, and it stalked forward, tilting its head to view her with one eye. Bat-like wings sprouted above its shoulders, grazing the studio walls. With a roar, the dragon charged past her at the plate glass, bursting through the windows. They exploded, sending cutting shards against Priya's face and eyelids. She spat slivers of glass from her mouth and wiped the blood off onto her hands.

When the glass stopped tinkling to the floor, she watched the creature sprint across the grass. It reached the beach and bounded into the sky.

Heavy as an iron rhino, it flew exempt from gravity. Glass crunched under her feet as Priya rushed to the window to watch it rise into the clouds and disappear. Injuries forgotten, her cheeks heated, and she glowed with happiness. With nothing but her own two hands, metal, and heat, she had brought a majestic creature to life.

Priya leaned through the broken window and cackled into the lashing rain. She gleefully rubbed her bloody hands together, brightened by strokes of lightning.

24

In the dark, Tonya concentrated on the sensation of each rung pressing into the arch of her foot to ward off dizziness as she climbed down the granite egg. At the bottom, she held up her phone and spotted the faint path through the trees that led to Betty's invisible staircase.

Without illusions to distract her, it was easier to climb in the dark, but the hermit was paranoid. Would Betty shoot if she heard noises outside her door?

On the deck, Tonya tried to detect dark magic. The granite egg was out of range, but something else tugged at her. Where? She slowly turned to locate the source which was somewhere behind Betty's house.

The wide deck wrapped around the house and stairs at the back led to the garden. Before Tonya could reach the grass, a board creaked underfoot. She froze, holding her breath to listen. Had Betty noticed her?

After long minutes, Tonya tiptoed down to a garden terraced into the hill. A light on the back of the house illuminated gentle slopes dropping away from a semi-circular lawn. Flat stones encircled a lily pond which sparkled beneath a string of tiny lights. Half of an enormous amethyst geode framed the pond from behind like a niche with a purple crystal halo. The effect was so magical, Tonya expected a fairy queen to dance on a lily pad. How could something so beautiful harbor death magic?

Footsteps approached.

Tonya dove behind the amethyst geode at the back of the pond and folded herself to fit behind it. She slowed her breathing.

Silence stretched. Tonya peeked out from behind the rock.

"Who's there?" Betty peered into the darkness, rifle in hand.

Tonya retreated, hoping Betty hadn't noticed her, but the recluse came around the rock and pointed the muzzle at her.

"Get out!"

Tonya dove to the right, raced across the lawn, and climbed to the veranda. Betty clomped after her in heavy boots and stopped.

Bang!

Tonya ran too slowly to put the house between her and Betty. Desperate to avoid gunfire, she lifted the screen off a bedroom window, went inside, and closed it behind her.

Betty's boots marched close by outside as Tonya crouched under the window. She was in a large bedroom with a pale pink spread. As she waited for Betty to leave, Tonya stared at a black-and-white photo on the wall of Betty standing by the lake with Len, Donna, Jack, and a skinny kid who looked familiar. Before Tonya could remember the connection, Betty thumped through the hallway.

Tonya flung open the bedroom window and dropped to the porch. The exterior lights would reveal her, so she sprinted around the building and through the garden. Behind the pond, she slipped into the trees at the top of the slope. There was no path down, but Tonya forged through the trees and groped her way down the hillside by phone flashlight. The ground fell away at a cliff with piles of rock and earth below. Finding a safer route, she picked her way slantwise down a steep grade, her shoes sliding in the sandy earth.

It took much longer at night, but she pushed between trees and through bushes to the stand of cedars where she'd stashed the Sea-Doo. At first, when she pulled on the tow rope, it wouldn't budge. Counterbalancing with all her weight, she tugged and dragged it to the water's edge.

Icy water stung her legs and thighs, but she didn't care. Tonya climbed onto the saddle, letting the craft drift. A waxing moon set sparkles rippling on the water behind her. Windows glowed from the far shore. She turned the key and sped toward the red bow lights of fishing boats strung like Christmas bulbs against the shimmery black lake.

Tonya's teeth chattered as the Sea-Doo glided shoreward, her eyes and ears straining for approaching boats. Safety demanded she drive slowly at night, but instinct shivered through her, urging her to flee, as a new, frigid energy radiated from deep below the surface.

Well, maybe not so deep.

Something rose bubbling under the hull and agitating the water. Looking straight down revealed a light-spangled surface with nothing but black below.

The water craft spun, knocking Tonya back in the saddle and yanking the tethered key out of the ignition. The engine cut out.

Regaining balance, Tonya replaced the key just as the water roiled up, tossing the Sea-Doo. The little craft bucked and swayed, soaking her clothes. Cursing, Tonya started the engine and steered away from whatever weirdness lurked in these waters. She needed to warn people.

As she reached for the phone in her glove box, a long pink tentacle wrapped itself around the handlebar and capsized the Sea-Doo. A sudden impact between her shoulder blades forced Tonya far under the water. Moments later, she bobbed to the surface, thankful for her lifejacket.

Her Sea-Doo had disappeared. In a short time, it couldn't have drifted far, but turning a full 360 degrees revealed nothing. It looked to have sunk, but that was impossible. The PWC was built to be unsinkable. The running lights should have announced its location, but she couldn't see it anywhere.

Shivering and with teeth chattering, Tonya had to give up on the Sea-Doo and admit she was in trouble. Wind and currents carried her farther from the island with each passing minute. Should she swim against the current back to shore? Before she reached land, the tentacles might grab her.

It was over two miles to the mainland. In the dark, a boat might hit her, but she'd be swimming with the waves and away from the creature.

Her lifeguard training dictated she swim the shorter distance back to the island, but they hadn't factored in the power of that tentacle! Tonya put her head down and swam for shore, listening for the whine of outboard motors. Fishers usually trolled slowly. She would hear the engine blades and dive out of the way in time.

Straining against the drag of the life preserver, the swim would take hours, and the boat rental would definitely charge her for losing the Sea-Doo, but at least she wasn't squid meat at the bottom of the lake.

That strange energy surged again ... It raised goosebumps on her arms, and she sprinted.

Too late. The depths exploded with glowing energy as something long and wiry wrapped around her ankle and dragged her down.

Down.

She descended blindly into the murky water. Her lungs burned. Instinct urged her to gulp air that was twenty feet out of reach—until a second tentacle wrapped itself around her chest, squeezing out the remaining breath in her lungs.

25

Tonya struggled out of sleep face down in the sand, spitting out grit. The last thing she remembered was using a key to stab a tentacle around her waist. On instinct, her right hand felt her pocket for a phone, but it was wet and useless.

Damp cave walls gleamed under halogen lights, revealing a tiny beach. It had to be the cave under Grand Island, accessible by an underwater tunnel. Tourists explored it with SCUBA equipment.

Metal scraped stone, and voices echoed through the tunnels. Had the tentacled creature captured more victims? She explored deeper into the cave, sprinting up a rocky mound.

At the top, she collided with a screaming girl whose face dripped with blood. The girl dodged Tonya and ran to the beach below, splashing into the water and shrieking.

Squinting into the bright lights, Tonya couldn't see what was chasing her.

"Cut! Cut!" a familiar voice ordered. "Come back and do it again."

Drake! She strained to see him in the dark. Zain, of the gravity-defying hair, trotted over the rock ledge wearing a steady cam rig on his chest. Instinctively, Tonya went toward Zain to give him a hug.

His look stopped her cold.

Of course. He couldn't remember her. It was dangerous for her to speak to any of the Digital Ninjas.

"A tentacled creature dragged me under. Do you know anything about that?" she asked, knowing full well that monster-obsessed Zain had to be involved.

"Nope." He couldn't meet her eye.

Just as she thought. She could just kill him if she wasn't so relieved to see him. Tonya couldn't have her friends back, but at least she knew they were alive.

Next over the rocky ridge appeared Drake, his eyebrow raised in an expression she'd seen a hundred times. She remembered his smiles too, and his strong arms pulling her close, and then she had to look away before she got choked up.

"I'm sorry," said Drake. "We were filming a remote-controlled squid."

"Giant squid," said Zain.

Drake shrugged. "It was supposed to look like it was attacking a swimmer."

"Me."

"Don't blame Petunia." Zain's hands went to his hips. "Her tentacles are just decorations."

"Your squid's name is Petunia?"

"Zain won the coin toss." Drake shrugged.

"If it wasn't your squid, what attacked me?"

Drake shot a look at Zain who glared back, arms crossed. "The remote control is working perfectly."

After Zain won the staring contest, Drake asked, "Are you okay?"

His brilliant blue eyes pulled Tonya in, but they could never date again, never be friends. If she triggered his memories, Donna would hard-wipe his mind and not care if she left him blank and drooling.

She changed the subject. "You're making a horror movie?" What else?

"The Great Canadian Horror Movie." Zain puffed out his skinny chest.

"Inspired by Margaret Atwood's essay "Survival." She couldn't help herself.

"How did you know?" Drake's gaze lingered. "I would remember meeting you."

If only. "Everyone's heard of the Digital Ninjas."

"Knew it!" Zain punched the air. "We're famous."

"Please tell me you found my Sea-Doo."

The girl who had run past Tonya returned wearing a cover-up. She wiped fake blood off her face with a damp cloth. "Sorry. I didn't see any Sea-Doo. I'm Grace, by the way."

"Nice to meet you." Tonya thought her face belonged on a movie poster.

"We've been filming all night, and I'm the only swimmer our squid was chasing."

"Then why did it attack me?"

"It's malfunctioning." She pointed to a swollen bruise on the side of Zain's head.

"Tentacle strike?"

Zain nodded. "She's ornery but worth it."

"We should help look for your Sea-Doo," Grace said.

"No time," said Zain. "We have three more scenes to shoot."

Drake pulled him aside whispering intensely.

When Zain returned, he led Tonya between a series of rocky mounds. The back of the cave opened to a cathedral ceiling illuminated by banks of lights that heated her face.

"What's that?" A boat shaped like a boot bobbed gently in the water near the shore. It was made of corrugated steel with a transparent dome on top.

"That's our monster." Zain tugged on her hand. "See the instrument panel? I designed the cockpit."

Drake joined them. "Priya did."

"She did the soldering." Zain sniffed. "It was my vision."

"You added tentacles on the back and nearly gummed up the motor."

"Where did you find the parts?" It didn't look waterproof to Tonya.

"When they put in new sewers," Drake said, "they left the old pipes lying around. That's what gave me the idea."

"But turning it into a monster was my inspiration." Zain doffed an imaginary cap and bowed.

"How deep does it go?"

"Twenty feet. The lake is shallow."

Zain's eyes lit up. "Except for one really deep spot near the tunnel into this cave."

The mini squid-sub had a marine compass, radio, dials, and controls Tonya had never seen before. Trust Drake to transform a giant discarded pipe into a sub, then use a cave as his film studio. In his own way, Drake was as creative as Priya.

Her gut ached remembering the good times with Drake and the Ninjas. After the bullies of high school, the Ninjas had rebooted her life and offered genuine friendship. She yearned to stay, but talking could spark dangerous memories. Council must not wipe Drake's sweet, sexy brain.

"How do I get out of here?"

"There's a back entrance." Zain led her higher up the sloping passageway to a pool of daylight on the cave floor where Grace was mounting fake tentacles on a boulder. Two rock sheets faced each other, leaving a gap barely twice Tonya's width. Overhead, a seagull flashed past, white against a rosy sunrise.

"I'd rather take the elevator," Tonya said.

"Nice one." Zain jumped onto the ladder and hung by his arms.

Grace put a hand on Tonya's shoulder. "It's solid. I've climbed it many times."

"I don't like heights," but Tonya couldn't swim back through the tunnel. Whatever had almost drowned her was strong and very much alive. She inhaled deeply and concentrated on slowly expelling her breath. If she looked calm and acted calm, maybe it would stop her heart from hammering.

"Take your time." Drake stood at her side, so calm and helpful.

Her nose tingled, and her eyes watered. "Thanks."

Maybe she held his gaze too long, because he frowned. Taking one last deep breath, she put her foot on the bottom rung and climbed.

Zain got on a few rungs below her, twitchier than a rabbit's nose. Could he wait patiently? Do monkeys stand in line for bananas?

The gap between the rock faces grew narrower near the top where the ladder rested at a ten-degree incline. A current of air blew hair in her face, and she stopped climbing.

"You okay?" Grace's voice echoed.

"We have a film to shoot. Quit messing around." Zain tapped the sides of the ladder, sending vibrations through to the soles of Tonya's sneakers.

"Come back." Drake took her hand and helped her off the ladder. "I'll take you home."

Was he that sweet with every girl? Despite herself, Tonya wished his concerned look was reserved for her alone.

"You almost drowned. That's enough trauma for one day." Grace put an arm around her. "Why don't we sit down for a minute? You want an iced tea, some water?"

"No more water!" said Zain.

"Sorry I'm such a wimp." Tonya's throat felt raw.

"Don't apologize." Grace sat beside Tonya on a flat rock and passed her a thermos of iced tea.

"I could drive you out in the sub," said Drake.

"What about my scene?" Zain asked.

"We can shoot a different scene until Drake comes back." Grace put her hands on her hips. "Right, Zain?"

"Yeah. I mean, I was just going to suggest that."

Tonya looked at Drake, and her pulse quickened. "It would just be us?"

"The sub's built for one," said Drake. "I hope you don't mind small spaces."

"Claustrophobia is not a problem."

But sitting so close to Drake? It was very wrong, but she didn't mind at all.

26

At the underwater beach, Tonya asked, "People don't use homemade subs. Are you sure it's safe?"

Drake picked up a line and pulled the sub to the beach. "An engineer looked over my plans. We tested it to fifty feet." He stepped onto the sub and opened the transparent dome. "Let me get in first."

"Is there only one seat?"

"Yeah." Zain had returned to see them off.

The sub bobbed as Drake threaded his muscular legs and torso through the upright section. "Don't worry. I'll keep you safe."

Drake's bright eyes looked innocent, but Tonya looked away. On a seat that small they'd be touching.

"Careful, it's wet." Drake's shoulders dwarfed the tiny cockpit as he extended a hand. "Step onto the front."

Under her foot the nose sank, and she slipped sideways until Drake steadied her.

"I'm going to start the motor. Come sit behind me."

Tonya shivered. Do. Not. Cry.

Without rocking the boat, Drake sat and extended his legs into the nose of the sub. "Ready?"

The electric engine hummed in neutral as Tonya slid in behind him. To leave a gap, she scrunched her tailbone backward against cold metal. It was bearable until she heard water rushing in. "What's happening?"

"We're taking on ballast to help us sink."

"How reassuring."

Drake drifted forward in neutral, their craft sinking until the dome reached water level. "Ready to dive?"

"Sure." Butterflies tickled her stomach as the nose dropped, and they glided through the tunnel.

"This is cool."

"Right?" Drake piloted smoothly using a joystick and foot pedals. His back radiated heat.

"Is it a tight squeeze?"

"Don't worry. I've been practicing."

She craved his arms around her, his face in her hair. Few girls meet their forever guy in their first year, but they had been making lifetime plans before Ashton Security erased his memories. To take her mind off his physical proximity, Tonya watched tiny algae balls rush into the cones of light made by their headlights. Outside the tunnel, they coasted over algae-fuzzed rocks and boulders sprouting zebra mussels.

"Do you want to stay underwater or ride along the surface?" Drake asked.

"Which is faster?"

"What's the rush? I bet you've never seen that before." He pointed to a school of fish grazing on a sunken canoe.

"Very interesting, but I'm in a hurry."

"What's wrong? Are you still feeling dizzy?"

"I'm fine."

"Of course, you've been through a lot." He adjusted the controls until the sub breached the surface and then accelerated.

Ever gallant, Drake would change some lucky girl's life. A lump caught in her throat. He didn't remember their first dance, their first kiss, the funny pop-up card he'd made to ask her out to their first dinner.

Tonya had eaten her next meal in jail.

It was too awful, sitting so close but unable to hold him or tell him about Helen.

"Are you crying?"

Tonya wiped her face. "Of course not."

"I saw you in the rearview mirror."

"I was thinking about my birth mother."

"Is she sick?"

"In jail." Now she'd said too much.

"We'll be at the beach soon. Then you can go see your mother." He stared at Tonya in the rearview. "Wait. I thought your aunt was sick."

"No."

"I know her."

"Doubt it."

He grinned. "Is her name Helen?"

Tonya clamped her mouth shut.

"Helen and Tonya. Tonya and Helen. I know you."

"No, you don't."

"And you and I " He twisted in his seat to look directly into her eyes. "Oh Tonya, I didn't even know I missed you." He folded her into his arms and tried to kiss her.

"Look out! There's a skier!"

"He's miles away." Correcting course, Drake asked, "Where have you been?"

"Jail mostly."

"No, really."

"Really."

"So, Helen is actually ..?"

"In jail, yeah, and you'll be in worse trouble if anybody finds out you remember me."

"Why?"

"City Council doesn't let outsiders know our secrets."

His crumpled brow went smooth as more memories fell into place. He steered in silence.

If he remembered her but not Waldock or magic—and the City Council never found out—maybe, just maybe, she could have him back. Her heart fluttered as she braced herself against the sub's sides.

Maybe the universe was kind and just. It would reunite them because they belonged together.

"I have to tell Zain."

Nope. The universe was a psycho with revenge fantasies.

They tied up at the dock, and while Drake brought his car around, Tonya went to face the boat rental owner. He would never believe how she lost the Sea-Doo. If she mentioned tentacles, he'd lose it.

The lights were on. "Hello?" Strange. On a Sunday morning in late June, someone should be working.

She walked through the empty shop and out the back door, where racks of paddle boards and kayaks stood undefended. Normally, when the shop was closed, the owner chained them together.

Back inside, pine stairs led to an empty roof patio. She leaned against the guardrail and contemplated the lake. The only sound was waves lapping softly. Where Shin had been varnishing the canoe sat an open can of sealant beside a dirty brush. Towels, coolers, umbrellas, and bags lay abandoned on the beach. She found Drake, who was backing up a trailer to the boat slip. "Where is everybody? Something's wrong."

Drake stared at the sand littered with cast-offs. "Must have rained."

"The sand looks dry."

Drake picked up a wallet in one hand and a purse in the other. "Something scared them away."

"It wasn't your mini-sub."

"The tentacles look pretty realistic."

"Whatever pulled me under the water was long and thin, like a long snake."

"We just crossed the lake, and I didn't see anything. Did you?"

"No." Tonya smelled woodsmoke, but the sky was clear the lake calm.

He inhaled deeply. "Do you think it was Waldock?"

"Who?" She played ignorant, her heart hammering in her chest.

"When I testified at the tribunal, Helen said Waldock's gang used to threaten people with fireballs."

"You remember everything." Tonya hugged him, and his soft bristles grazed the skin around her mouth as they kissed, tickling her. Eventually they broke apart, and Tonya checked over her shoulder for witnesses.

"It's good to have you back." Tears welled in her eyes, so she buried her face in his chest to hide them. "Nobody can see us together. If we meet, pretend to be strangers."

"Never. What if I forget you again?" He brushed a stray hair from her forehead.

She stepped out of his arms. "The memory charm blocks you from retrieving memories. It doesn't erase them. The first time, anyway. If they erase your memory twice, it damages the brain."

"We should report them."

"Loon Lake has its own laws. And the Ninjas can never know anything about this, for their own protection."

"I smell fire."

Tonya told him about the fire at the campground.

"Can Waldock return from the dead again?"

"I don't think so, but I'm still learning. I have to study magic in the catacombs under City Hall."

"Secret catacombs? Zain would have a geek-gasm."

"You can't tell him, and we have bigger problems. Whatever dragged me underwater wasn't Waldock. And now it's cleared the beach. Maybe it hurt people."

Drake took out his phone. "I'm calling the police."

"Don't bother." Tonya checked the Old Family News app. "Somebody already called them, but there's no mention of a creature. They claim the disturbance was a waterspout, but they're calling all witnesses to give a statement in person."

"So City Council can wipe their memories?"

"Exactly. Then Ashton Security will hunt down any leftover witnesses."

"So, you're saying there's a big monster in the lake, and City Council is covering it up?"

"Yup."

"But calling the police will get our minds erased?"

"Welcome to Loon Lake."

"That is so wrong."

Tonya laughed.

He frowned.

"Sorry. I'm just happy you're still you."

For the first time in months, she wasn't alone. In October, Drake had faced Waldock without fear, and she trusted him utterly. He might not know magic, but with Drake beside her, she could face anything. Except hurting him.

"There's nothing you can do. Walk away and pretend you don't know me."

"Not going to happen."

"I mean it. Threaten the Old Families, and you'll find yourself wandering the highway with a headache, an empty wallet, and no memory of the past five years."

Drake's face sagged, and she yearned to kiss the hurt away. He asked, "When can I see you again?"

"Never. You can't know people like me."

"They can't separate us. I need you."

His voice was too loud. People might hear. Tonya steered Drake behind the rental shop. "They didn't erase your memory just to keep our secrets. Donna Ashton hates my family, so she attacked my friends. And now she has more power as acting mayor, and folks won't oppose her for fear of being banished."

"That sounds medieval."

"Worse. When you get banished, they wipe years from your memory and cast a curse that blocks you from returning. For the rest of your life, your eyes slide over any road that leads here. No one makes it back." Except for Helen, but she had banished herself before the Council could do it officially.

"You want me to pretend I don't remember you?"

"No, forget me."

"Never."

"No texts or calls. Zero contact. Promise?" She yearned for one last kiss, a proper goodbye.

The way he couldn't meet her eyes made Tonya's stomach flip. They stood closer. Without thinking, Tonya leaned in, and Drake stole a chaste kiss, barely a brush of the lips.

"I'll never forget you," he whispered.

Her body responded, and he moved closer, intent on deepening the kiss, but Tonya backed out of his embrace.

Blinking away tears, Tonya sprinted away until her sprint turned into a steady run. There was only one thing to do. Her strides lengthened and grew powerful. There was a way to fix this, but she couldn't do it alone. She had to free Helen and restore her powers.

Her birth mother could combine and direct magical energies with Tonya's help, and Helen had plenty of spells. One of them had to be strong enough to tear Loon Lake away from Donna Ashton.

27

MONDAY MORNING, TONYA PULLED her phone out of the rice bag where she'd left it to dry overnight. When she switched it on, it worked! Finally, her luck was turning.

Humming to herself, she showered and chose a respectable outfit. The entity she needed to consult after school would expect formal courtesy. Anything less would bring down its wrath. It felt weird pulling on a skirt and blouse before magic class, but this time she wouldn't have to shovel muck afterward.

Strangely, Marta didn't tease Tonya about her dressy attire or anything else. From the moment Arjun arrived, she grabbed him for the hands-on magic session, whispering in his ear and giggling.

Smitten? Marta? Nah. To admit that would be to admit she was human.

The Mods partnered up, leaving her odd one out. Maybe it was better that way. As long as she wore the anklet, she couldn't use magic. All that remained was to watch, learn, and memorize against the day they allowed Tonya to use her powers.

That was the hope, until her father's text snuffed it out:

Fading Times: Mayor falls deeper into coma. By-election announced.

That afternoon, lightning failed to strike Tonya as she entered City Hall, but her neck prickled with loose psychic energy. You could practically smell Donna's allies casting spells behind closed doors, and with the mayor gone, nobody could stop them.

Tonya went for her only remaining weapon. Research. City Hall housed the Old Families' secret tribunal and local records dating back to the European settlers. With Helen's hearing the following Monday, time to clear her was running out. Betty's photo with Waldock was a clue. They had hung out together, and Tonya was determined to find proof in the archives. There had to be a yearbook or photos of the young Mods who cast spells on the island. One of them might have killed Waldock the first time, and if she could prove it, the tribunal would have to free Helen.

But first, she needed to convince the Librarian to help.

A mosaic of the Three-Century Ash graced the elegant dome that Tonya passed under. It symbolized ancient powers watching over them. At least, it had until Tonya burned down the sacred tree, destroying their protection.

On the long nights in her cell, regret had besieged Tonya as she tossed on her cot. If only she hadn't burned down the Three-Century Ash and turned Loon Lakers against her. Its absence let her enemies see through the charms hiding the Staff of Storms and use it to subdue her birth mother. Without the tree to absorb and purify death magic, any number of nasty spirits could lurk in their cemetery.

But it wasn't entirely her fault. If Helen had revealed Tonya's parentage and taught her to use magic, they might have teamed up sooner. But she hadn't, and now Tonya had to uncover Waldock's murderer alone.

Tonya's steps slowed on the marble floor. Donna had summoned the National Council of Magic Users to try Helen. According to the witch's advocate, National sided with those in power. If Tonya couldn't refute Donna's accusations, they would find Helen guilty and execute her.

The information desk looked abandoned, but she knew better. Tonya had heard descriptions of the Librarian's lace bonnet and prim floor-skimming skirts. Talk about old school. Tonya peered over the counter and cleared her throat.

No response.

"Anybody here? I need to see the Librarian."

A draft shivered down her back like a ghostly presence. Still, nothing materialized behind the counter. A polite ghost would let Tonya see her.

"Hello?"

The logbook rushed at Tonya across the counter, followed by a floating pen. She snatched it out of the air and filled in her details.

Name: Tonya Jones

Purpose: Looking for records mentioning Jack Waldock, 1980-2000.

She pushed the book back across the counter.

Time passed, but nothing happened. Was the Librarian shunning Tonya for personal reasons, or had the City Council ordered it? Tonya lifted her pant leg to check the ankle monitor. It wasn't warm or glowing. Could it suppress her ability to see ghosts? No, it didn't work on the phantom newsboy.

A book floated out of the back room and thudded onto the counter. Another followed, and another, plus a stack of yellowed newspapers bound with twine.

"Thank you," Tonya told the chilly air.

The Librarian didn't reply, so Tonya lifted the stack of books.

Icy hands grabbed her wrists. "Let go!"

A pen tapped angrily on the register as frosty air blasted her face.

"What now?"

A new piece of paper materialized on top of the sign-out book:

Dear Library Patron,

Treat Old Family documents with respect. Turn pages using a pencil and wear cotton gloves while reading. The fine for damaged materials shall not be waived. To resolve your fine, life energy, in the precise amount needed to heal the damaged volume, will be withdrawn from the borrower. This painful process typically shortens the human lifespan, so do take care of the books.

Have a pleasant day!

Tonya brought the books and receipt with her, balancing the stack against her chest as she walked back to the dorm.

Crossing the foyer, a girl sped toward her, carrying two large coffees. It happened slowly but too fast. The girl tripped and pitched forward, arms outstretched. She must have squeezed her hands, because the lids opened, spraying coffee in an expanding plume headed for the books.

Except Tonya spun, taking the hot coffee spray on her back.

"I'm so sorry." The girl rushed over, flapping a napkin as if it could wave away the coffee. "I'll pay your cleaning bill."

"Don't worry about it." Tonya had protected the books and could hardly wait to open them.

Back inside her dorm room, she spread the materials on her rickety study desk and untied the cord binding the newspapers. The top one was full of ads, articles, and team scores from twenty years ago. Tonya scanned headlines for suspicious events around the time Helen and Waldock were seeing each other. That is, if you considered sucking death magic out of corpses dating.

In Mundane hands, stories in the *Loon Lake News* appeared innocuous. Touched by a magic user, *The Fading Times* appeared, and a new set of headlines revealed themselves. At least, they should. After so many years, the spell had faded.

Helen could have charmed the paper into giving its secrets willingly, and Tonya itched to push power into the fading spell, but her anklet forbade it.

Concentrating so as not to channel magic, Tonya let her guard down enough to sense what power remained. The print blurred and refocused into pale wavering text describing a fire on the island the year Waldock disappeared. The editorial complained that the City Council refused to confront a gang of magic-using hooligans who were terrorizing law-abiding citizens with fireballs. Greedy for every detail, Tonya read quickly, racing against the waning power of the spell.

The text faded before she could finish, and the paper burst into flames that licked her face. The smell of burning hair filled her nostrils, and she choked as she dropped the paper and stomped out the fire.

A singed page curled at the edge and waggled victoriously. The Librarian had set a trap that could cost her years of life.

Longingly, she eyed the stack of publications that tempted her with the promise of clues. She yearned to search through the materials, but Tonya refused to let the Librarian beat her.

Time to interview survivors from Waldock's hooligan days.

28

BEHIND CITY HALL, A cement wall screened the jail entrance from passersby. Tonya had been released through this gate, thanks to Helen.

Tonya's fingers trembled on the intercom button. "Tonya Jones to visit Helen Fitzpatrick."

"We know."

The gate buzzed open and a skinny guard in Ashton Security gray brought her through the door and made her walk ahead of him to a counter. Tonya stood behind a line on the floor while the bored attendant took her valuables. Tonya knew the routine. Surrender your phone and purse. Get x-rayed. Submit to scanning with a magic-detection wand. Sign forms.

Wait.

Wait.

Wait.

At last, the attendant waved her through, and the guard marched Tonya down a steep flight of steps into the catacombs under City Hall. Stepping into the white-tiled hallway raised the hair on Tonya's neck as she felt the Staff of Storms extinguish her powers. She should be used to it after Professor Kirkdene's tour, but without magic the force went out of her legs, and she suddenly craved a coffee. Or a nap.

"In there." The guard's voice grated on Tonya's ears. "Speak through the bars."

"What, no visitor's area? No day pass to the gardens?"

The guard's frown didn't thaw.

The Staff of Storms broke Helen's telepathic link, so they whispered while the guard stared at the opposite wall listening in on every word.

"I looked through newspapers from the time Waldock disappeared for three days. You were on the island and dating him when it happened. What aren't you telling me?"

"I broke up with Jack after he tricked me into channeling death magic. Len was delighted."

"Why?"

"Jack used to be Loon Lake's Golden Boy. Son of the mayor and a rascal, but destined for power. It didn't matter how many exams he flunked or how many classes he skipped, his dad bailed him out. His mediocre marks got him into business college so he could work in his dad's office, future assured. The Waldocks were a political dynasty. All Len had was a gang of losers."

"Why did Waldock tolerate him?"

"Len enticed him with power. Rebellion. Jack craved attention and yearned to prove he was more than the mayor's son. He loved to impress me." She sighed.

"I can't believe it. You still have feelings for him?"

"No." Her voice softened. "But the real Jack Waldock could've had any girl, and he chose me."

"What happened on the island?"

"We went to do magic in secret. Len brought a gym bag full of occult stuff and made a big deal of not opening it."

"Who was with you?"

"Jack, Len, Ran, and Betty, Luke, and a few other teens. The girls told their parents they were having a sleepover, and we took a boat after dusk."

"How could Len do death magic outside the cemetery?"

"There was a death."

Heavy footsteps alerted Tonya to Miranda's approach. "How was your first class?" Her parole officer knew how much she'd dreaded going.

"I got through it."

"Did the ankle bracelet chafe with sport socks on?" That had been Miranda's parting advice before she let Tonya leave prison.

"It's fine."

"Sorry about this. Donna's orders." Raising her hands, Miranda pushed a wave of energy at the cell which pushed Helen back from the bars. Tonya could see her speaking, but her voice was muffled. When Tonya reached through the cell bars, an invisible barrier hard as ice stopped her hand.

"Helen!"

"Time's up."

The lanky guard leaped to his feet, and Tonya could barely wave goodbye before he bulldozed her out.

29

Sunshine lit the gardens behind City Hall as Tonya left the prison. Beds of orange lilies crowded near the greenhouse. If she wanted to free Helen before the lilies stopped blooming, Tonya needed to find clues. Hoping the local high school might have a yearbook listing Helen's classmates, Tonya turned up Main Street but got stuck behind a parade.

Baton twirlers led the Loon Lake High marching band. Clowns danced on stilts, and people blew whistles and banged pots filling the street.

"Now that's some show!" The phantom newsboy shimmered into view.

"Ahh!" She jumped. "Who are you?"

"Johnny the Scoop. Like my pen name?"

"Sure, but you shouldn't side with the Ashtons. They made the mayor sick, and now Donna is gunning for his job."

"If it's news, I cover it."

"Helen is in jail for a crime she didn't commit. That deserves your attention."

"Boring. Your family is relevant like last year's forecast. This is the future of Loon Lake." He raised a glowing hand to point at Donna.

Interesting. To get rid of Johnny, she simply had to make herself boring. Turning her body, she sidled to the front of the crowd. A pair of six-foot guys let her stand in front, no charm from Helen required. Their kindness made her want to hug them when so many townsfolk did their best to shun her.

Atop the float, from glossy red fingertips, Donna released handfuls of candy into the crowd. They fell in a sparkling shower, lighting the citizens' faces with ecstasy.

Johnny passed through Tonya, making her shiver. "Now that's a parade!"

Tonya trembled. "Look at their faces. She's casting a spell on the crowd."

"They look happy."

"Like kids-with-a-new-puppy happy. It isn't natural for them to look overjoyed, and you know it."

"Mods like to show off their powers, and Ashton supporters like magic." He chewed the back of a phantom pencil. "I don't see the harm."

"Confusing people's minds better not be permanent."

"You're twitchier than a chipmunk. Relax." He set up an ancient, semi-transparent camera and squeezed a bulb on a cord to ignite the flash. The camera was an antique like its owner, frozen in the past like the staff of *The Fading Times*.

"Kid, let me speak to your editor."

"Not a chance. If I bring him your problems, I can kiss my promotion goodbye."

"Not if I grant you an exclusive he won't believe."

"Like what?"

"I'll go on the record and spill everything. Helen, Mom, their volcanic feud. It's soap opera powerful."

"Sorry, doll. Your parents are boring, but I'll be there taking shorthand the next time you screw up."

The float left the road and stopped at a small park. Donna picked up a loud hailer to address the crowd.

"Citizens of Loon Lake, it's time for a change. A vote for me isn't blanket support for one faction. I will promote a peaceful future in which Mods, Trads, and Pures live in harmony."

Heck, if Tonya didn't know better, she'd vote for Donna herself. How was it possible an extreme Mod, who had flouted the anti-magic policies of Loon Lake for years, was preaching harmony and compromise?

"Mods know they must be responsible. Vote for balance in Loon Lake. If we win, the changes will be barely noticeable. Mods will gain the freedom to practice magic and to teach your children to control it, but not at the expense of their neighbors' peace of mind."

"This is a trick! Donna won't restrain her supporters. The point of electing her is so Mods can use magic freely."

"That's my scoop," said Johnny. "The Ashtons have developed a spell that enters voter's minds and detects what they most desire."

"Like an opinion poll?"

"That's primitive Mundane tech. Donna's spell creates a custom message in the mind of each voter. She can stand on the platform and declare up is down and down is up, but unless that's what you want, you won't hear it."

"I heard her perfectly. She wants to bring order to magic use and peace to Loon Lake."

"Because that's what you need. You're a pariah, and so is your mother. Your desperate desire is for folks to accept everybody, because that's the only way they'll accept you."

The spook left, rudely walking through Tonya's body, and leaving her chilled.

30

In the hallway, Priya heard a murmur of conversation and student laughter. Intuition drew her to the common room between the wings of her dorm, where three varsity hockey teammates played video games on the couch. It was a strange sensation, but not like the nudge her subconscious gave her when an art project was going the wrong way. This intuition felt like magic, a spell cast on her feet that drove them to this room.

But why? And where did this urge come from?

Priya sank into an upholstered chair and watched the future graduates demolish each other in a clichéd battle royale. These were the leaders of tomorrow, hooting over digital explosions?

In the kitchen, a cluster of young women gathered at the counter, eating popcorn and subtly checking out the gamers. There was a microwave, sink, and a few cupboards with plates, but no food in them. For good reason. At midnight, hungry students attacked unguarded nibbles faster than zombies ate brains.

Magic tingled here, like when Roberto made energy to flow through her. What an oddball. Guys hit on her all the time, but his attentions weren't ordinary flirtation. His obsession with her dreams, the way he knew too much about her … in the moment it had felt good, but in retrospect, Roberto set off her creep alarm.

And the nightmares she'd been having? They were his fault, too. The one where her sculpture came alive and smashed through the studio window felt so real, she'd checked for damage the morning after.

On the kitchen wall, a bulletin board shimmered into existence. The women didn't react, even though two were facing it. Was she trapped in yet another dream? Lately, there had been too many.

Priya blinked, but the cork board remained, sprouting flyers and pinned notes. She approached, expecting the object to fade like an illusion. Slowly, Priya ran her finger along the cold aluminum frame of the impossible cork board.

"Ouch!" Blood sprang from a cut on her finger. She had nicked herself on the unfinished edge. "Who knew magic stuff was so cruddy?"

"I'm sorry, what?" The student wore short pigtails and a Blue Jays shirt.

"I cut my finger."

"Want a Band-Aid? I have one in my room."

Priya sucked blood off her finger. "No thanks, but was this here before?"

The girl stared at the wall where Priya was pointing. "Was what there?"

The others had stopped watching the guys and turned their attention to Priya.

"Nothing."

"It was an ant, wasn't it?" The girl traced a finger down the kitchen wall, her hand passing through the cork board like it was a ghost. "They get into everything, and now I find out they bite!" Her panicked voice drew the other girls closer.

"Don't worry, it wasn't an ant. I must have given myself a paper cut."

"On the wall?"

"Maybe I did it earlier and just noticed now." The tip of her finger looked fine. Had it been a hallucination?

"Thanks anyway." Somebody must have slipped something into her tea. When she found out who, she was going to break the spectral bulletin board over their head. She tugged at the corner, but it wouldn't budge.

Cards pinned to the board glowed like pastel beacons. One offered tutoring for Kirkdene's class, whoever he was. Another advertised an enchanted Frisbee for sale. The brightest card sought a part-time gopher/ receptionist for City Hall Library. Crazy as it seemed, the magic corkboard job would pay enough for her extra sculpting materials. When she plucked it off the board, the card's light blinked out, as if it had overheard her thoughts and knew its job was done.

Excited to be chosen by a magical card, she rushed back to her room, printed off a resume, threw on her interview suit, and drove her aging Toyota, Baby, to City Hall.

Near the city center, breezes rolled off the lake carrying humidity and a hint of rotting fish. From the far side of the lot, she crossed the sizzling pavement and ducked into the entrance. Priya patted her chignon into place as her eyes adjusted to the dim light filtering through a skylight at the peak of the cupola. Looking up to appreciate the mosaic, Priya gazed at a giant tree surrounded by fierce women in cloaks. How nice to see herstory included in town history.

The reception counter stood empty.

"Hello?" Priya rang the bell. No answer.

Brandishing her resume like a passport, she stepped around the counter into the office. It looked empty, but somebody cleared their throat. "I'm here for the job."

Nobody appeared. Odd. She felt a presence but saw no one.

"Well, aren't you a gutsy young thing?"

The voice by her ear made Priya jump. Her senses screamed that someone stood beside her, close enough to touch. She reached for the voice.

"No, you don't!" Chill air ruffled past Priya's hair. "One does not prod a lady like a piece of fruit."

"Is this a joke? Come out, Zain! I'm talking to a hidden speaker, aren't I?"

Except Zain didn't answer. Nobody was laughing, and air brushed past her ankles like the ruffle of skirts. Something feathery skimmed her cheek. "Ugh!"

"Don't be afraid." The aged woman's voice came out of the air. The resume trembled in Priya's hands.

"Where are my manners? Let me introduce myself."

As the invisible thing approached, Priya backpedaled, stumbling into the shelf behind her.

"There's no reason to stamp and snort. You'll find few job vacancies in Loon Lake."

"Fair point." Rows of bookshelves filled the cramped room, but there was no camera, no speakers. The hairs raised on Priya's neck didn't lie. There was a presence in the room.

The voice intoned, "I am the Librarian."

Willing it to stop shaking, she thrust her hand into the void. "Priya, pleased to meet you. Did you send the magic bulletin board?"

"Yes."

"You're a ghost."

"Nothing escapes your keen mind."

"How can I work for someone I can't see?"

"Most find my looks unpleasant." The temperature dropped, and ozone scented the room like gathering rain. A firm grip enclosed Priya's hand, cold and hard as bone. At last, the thing released her.

"You'll need both hands to gather up that jaw you dropped." A dark chuckle rang in Priya's ears. "It's been so long since I met a greenhorn. I've forgotten how amusing it is."

"Why can't I see you?" Priya retrieved her resume from the ground.

"Let's just say I'm hard of appearing."

"Which is why you need a receptionist." A steady paycheck would buy a lot of steel. "I'm your girl."

"How casual." Invisible hands tugged the resume away. "Sit." Bookshelves covered every wall, and three overloaded desks filled the office. "Come girl, sit. I have appointments after yours."

Priya dropped into a chair.

The ghostly presence clucked its tongue. "You feel my presence, a rare talent for an outsider. Explain yourself. Why can you hear me? Whence do you hail?"

In Toronto, racist strangers asked where she came from. It felt surreal to be asked by an empty chair. "Toronto."

"Your family?"

"I'm from a family of five."

"And?"

"I'm the only artist. My older siblings are engineers." Priya bit her lower lip. "I want to be a sculptor. I'm not sure how that relates to the job."

"Why can you sense me? Few outsiders have this gift."

"Outsiders from Toronto?"

"People from anywhere but Loon Lake. I'm aware your ancestors aren't from this continent."

"Are yours?"

"We are all settlers on Aboriginal lands. My ancestors go back three hundred years to the Old Families."

Priya pictured a European in a long dress and bonnet. "My people are from India, but I'm from Toronto."

"What skills have you?"

"I can type business letters, file, and update websites. I've operated multi-line phone systems and can speak three languages."

"Trifles. Show me what you can do."

"I don't understand."

"Energy collects around you. This place likes you, but I don't know why. Show me your powers."

"I don't have any."

"Hmm."

"I'm good at art." Priya itched to see her interviewer's reaction.

"And?"

"I make sculptures in steel and animatronics. Those are sculptures that move with motors inside. Did you hear about my giant tarantulas in the cemetery?"

The Librarian chuckled dryly. "I prefer to hear it from the horse's mouth. What is the point of your art? Where is the magic?"

"Art lets me share feelings. My dream is to turn pro, so I'm renting studio time this summer."

"Laudable, but why not just use magic?"

"I can't."

"Who taught you to channel power?"

"I don't."

"I've heard enough."

The chair scraped back so Priya stood, directing her eyes to where the woman's head *should* be. When she held out her hand to shake, an icy grip squeezed it.

"If chosen, you will hear from us soon."

Priya nodded long enough for politeness, then rushed past the counter and strode across the wide marble floor. Outside, the sun warmed her skin, and she could breathe normally. She had talked to a ghost!

Priya got into Baby and gripped the blistering hot steering wheel. There probably was no job. The ghostly Librarian just wanted to freak out the newcomer. Let her try. They could spook her all they liked. She wasn't leaving Loon Lake without finishing her masterpiece.

31

PRIYA'S STOMACH GROWLED ON the way back to campus, so she pulled into the grocery store. In the parking lot, two tykes squabbled over a box of sugary cereal until their mother snatched it over their heads.

Déjà vu.

On this spot, she had witnessed the same conflict before. But when...?

Priya hurried into the store, goosebumps prickling, as if the quarreling children portended doom. Inside, boxes, bottles, and jars packed the shelves, but another set of images haunted the space. Empty shelves. Broken glass. People fighting for scraps. Was it a dream or had she witnessed it?

Priya grabbed a bag of chips and fled to the checkout.

The cashier's face triggered a memory of the same woman moaning, her eyes milky and blind. This was no déjà vu. The store was possessed. She raced for the parking lot into the path of a car.

Too late to jump.

Four thousand pounds of metal hurtled toward her. The driver's mouth dropped open, and Priya watched in slow motion as his eyebrows raised, his hands lifting from the wheel to shield his face. Tires screeched.

The bumper nudged her leg, and the horn blared.

"Idiot!" The driver pulled a U-turn and raced off.

She stumbled across the lot, strapped herself into Baby and sat back to catch her breath. Zombies. Food-crazed zombies had shuffled through this grocery store. Was her vision a memory or a dream? She grasped at fleeting images in the recesses of her mind.

The Librarian's interrogation was making her paranoid. Besides, soon she would complete sculpting the beast. Then she could retreat to Toronto, where the only grocery store zombies groaned and shuffled because of post-party hangovers.

32

At dawn, Priya woke to seagull cries against a pink sky, her back chaffing against damp sand. She pulled herself into the lotus position and contemplated the beach in front of the studio. Why was she outside instead of sleeping on the studio cot? There had been another thunderstorm last night, and nothing could have convinced her to sleep outside. The last thing she remembered was standing on a ladder, blowtorch in hand, soldering her dragon.

Her eye rested on two sets of lizard footprints that led out of the water and disappeared into the grass. She squinted at the tracks, which were reminiscent of the salamander prints Roberto had shown her, except they were huge. A line divided the prints, as if a stegosaurus and its mate had walked out of the water dragging their tails.

It had to be an elaborate prank played by bored summer students. But if so, why choose this obscure strip of muddy sand?

The pink sky brightened, and the riverbanks wouldn't stay deserted for long. She texted Arjun:

Weird request. Help me find a giant lizard? RN. At art studio.

Except it was summer, and her pal liked his sleep. It could be hours before Arjun stirred. Who else could she count on?

Palms sweaty, she watched for movement as she texted Drake.

He replied immediately.

On my way.

After sleeping on the beach, she probably looked like a scarecrow. Priya dashed into the studio to look in the mirror. Her hair stood out on one side. She tugged a big hairbrush through knots and twigs, releasing showers of sand. With a clean rag, she scrubbed her face, then threw on a spare shirt and painting pants. To convince Drake giant amphibians existed, it was best to look calm, clean, and sober.

She was fastening her ponytail with a lace scrunchie when Drake arrived. If he noticed the circles under her bloodshot eyes, his smile didn't waver.

"Come see." She led him to the beach.

At the sound of their approach, a curvy student in pink fled for the trees, her long snowy hair flapping like a truce flag.

"Come back!" Drake shouted, but the young woman disappeared around the corner of the studio.

"Do you know her?"

Drake hurried after the stranger while Priya reassured herself the mystery girl hadn't erased the prints. She needed to know they were real, despite recent lapses. Talking to an invisible librarian? Remembering a grocery store apocalypse? Nearly walking into a car? Something was wrong with her brain.

Priya kneeled to touch the footprint. The molded sand didn't feel like a hallucination, so what was it? A campus prank? Maybe, but what kind of prankster would choose this narrow, unpopular stretch of beach? It defied logical sense. Which meant going beyond logic. In Loon Lake, once you eliminated the impossible, what remained was magic. Like the frosty-eyed grocery store rioters.

Memories flooded back. Drake had been there.

Where was he going?

Priya spotted Drake beside the building, arguing with the stranger in pink. The young woman's long white hair looked wrong, but her face seemed familiar.

A wave of nausea rose, but when Priya looked away, her stomach settled.

Weird. She tried looking again.

Same reaction. Her tummy revolted whenever she looked at the stranger.

Leaving the two of them to their argument, Priya went inside for supplies. Something was messing with her memory, but she'd give them a fight. Nobody was going to make her forget the lizard prints. She slammed open cupboards and dumped her materials into buckets.

Minutes later, with a large pail of wet plaster of Paris in hand, she smoothed her stride to keep the liquid from sloshing. On her knees, she poured plaster into the largest print before Drake returned with his blushing friend.

"Priya, this is Tonya."

"Hi." Priya waved, then moved to cast the next print, keen to finish before the rising sun dried the sand.

"Told you she wouldn't recognize me." Tonya whispered to Drake. "This is a terrible idea." Tonya pulled away from Drake.

"Wait." Drake put a hand on her shoulder, an intimate touch.

"Do I know you?" Priya's nausea rose, then faded.

"It's a long story. What made these prints?"

"Looks like it was a dinosaur the size of a car. I'd leave if I were you, in case it comes back."

"Sensible, even when facing the incredible." She beamed at Priya like a proud parent.

Priya scrutinized the stranger. Tonya looked Priya's age, but she dressed like a kid in pink sweatpants and running shoes. Wait. A memory stirred. Hadn't she bought a pair of pink sweats at the campus bookstore? As a gift? For a close friend?

Drake interrupted her thoughts. "Do you remember?"

"You were there." Priya pointed at Tonya. "The Halloween installation, the cafeteria riot ... police locked down campus and then " She looked to Drake to fill in the blanks.

"My memory was blocked too, until I met Tonya." He hugged the girl and kissed her cheek. "Love never forgets."

Priya's memories flowed back. "Tonya! It's me." She flung her arms open for a hug.

"I know." Tonya didn't move.

"Aren't you happy?"

"No, forget me."

"Why?"

Tonya showed Priya the anklet linking her to the Staff of Storms. "Ashton Security will wipe your mind if they find out you remember anything, and Donna Ashton will enjoy doing it because she hates me."

"There are giant lizards on the loose. How can people stay safe if they don't know about magic?"

"That's Ashton Security's job."

"You just said the Ashtons hate you."

"And all my friends. You can't be seen with me. Go, both of you. I'll deal with whatever made those prints."

33

IN THE STUDIO, FLOOR-TO-CEILING windows gave an unobstructed view of clear skies and boats on the lake. Watching for rogue lizards, Tonya called the mayor's office. The receptionist laughed when she described the mega footprints and refused to direct her call.

With her reputation for trouble, it didn't surprise her.

After she hung up, Priya said, "We should call the police."

"An ordinary officer will answer the phone. When I describe giant lizard footprints, he'll think I'm on drugs."

"We can't just ignore them."

"Giant lizards don't scare me. My concern is the lack of reaction." Tonya showed Priya her phone. "Yesterday, a beach full of sunbathers disappeared, but there was no mention on the Old Family News app. City Council knows, and they're covering it up."

"Do you know that guy, Roberto, who works in the bakery? He slipped something into my tea, and since then I've been having visions." Priya emphasized with her hands. "Last night, it felt like I was having nightmares, but he's behind it. He called himself a catalyst and directed power through me. He used me to make giant lizards. If people get hurt, it'll be partly my fault for letting him take advantage of me."

"There's only one group who can handle it."

"The Digital Ninjas?" Priya asked.

"No, we need to call in the specialists." Tonya knew the number in by heart. It was the same number for her parole officer, Miranda.

A deep voice answered. "Ashton Security."

It sounded like Donna's older brother, Marvin, the accountant. Skinny and quiet, in grade school, kids used to mock his hand-me-downs and ink-stained pockets. Today, Marvin sported khakis and $300 golf shirts.

"I'd like to report giant lizards." Tonya picked up a pen.

"Who is this?"

"They crawled out of the lake onto campus." She watched the window for monsters. "Their footprints are enormous. Promise you'll look into it."

"This must be Tonya Jones, or should I say Fitzpatrick?"

"Correct. Send some guards to search the university grounds before somebody gets hurt."

"Pranking us won't help your mother's cause."

Priya gestured at the window. "Look."

Tonya hung up. "What?"

"That weird kid is staring at us."

"Where?"

"Look down. See him resting his grubby fingers against the window?"

"I don't see anyone." Priya was pointing at nothing. "Wait, is he wearing a cap? Short pants like Oliver Twist?"

"You know him?"

Tonya stormed out the door and addressed the spot Priya had described. "I know you're here. Show yourself!"

Priya caught up. "What's your name, little boy?"

"You can see him?" She was an outsider.

"We won't hurt you." Priya's voice was softer than the brat deserved.

When Johnny shimmered into view, Tonya yearned to grab him by his translucent lapels. "Stop spying on me!"

"Can't a fella do his job? Forgive me for trying to break a story."

"Somebody put you up to this. Ghosts don't wander all over the countryside. They haunt one place or stay in the cemetery."

"Ever heard of a roving reporter? I go where I like." He sniffed ostentatiously. "I have a nose for news, and you stink like a story."

Priya smiled gently. "Where's your family?"

The urchin shrugged. "You're destined for great things, Miss Priya. Once I've wrapped up Tonya's story, grant me an exclusive?"

His tone was flirty, but Tonya didn't have time for it. "Who helped you escape the cemetery?"

"I don't reveal my sources, especially to you."

"What do you have against Tonya?" Priya smiled and kneeled to his level. "Come here. I've never hugged a ghost before." Over her shoulder she mouthed, "Adorable."

"Forget it. I'm a tough guy, see?"

"You know you want to." Priya flung her arms wide.

"All right toots, but don't let it go to your head." He rushed up to Priya and planted a loud kiss on her lips.

"Hey!"

"That was just a taste. I'm very popular with the ladies." He dusted the front of his shirt modestly.

Tonya whispered to Priya, "Find out who set this ghoul to spy on me."

"It's rude to whisper, and I'm not a ghoul."

"Sorry," said Priya. "They trust you with the big stories, don't they?"

He nodded and rocked on his heels. "With a scoop this big, the editor will give me a front-page headline in *The Fading Times*."

"*Fading Times?*" Priya asked.

"The dead folks' daily." His hand panned across an imaginary headline. "Your news for life, after life. Great tagline, right? Someday, I'll be editor-in-chief."

"I'm sure you will." Priya coaxed him with a smile. "So, who sent you to watch Tonya?"

Johnny scuffed his semi-transparent shoes. "Can't tell you, miss." He started to fade.

"Tell me, or I'll tell the Librarian you left the cemetery and started spying on the living."

The boy's eyes widened. "You wouldn't."

"Try me. She just gave me a job."

"I can't tell you. He'll finish me." The boy's image flickered.

Priya tilted her head. "Who?"

"He'll dig up my grave."

"Please." Priya clasped her hands. "He's putting people in danger."

"How exactly?" From the pocket of his ratty jacket, he pulled out a glowing pen and pad.

"You tell us first," Tonya insisted. "Who are you reporting to?"

"Promise not to tell I spilled the beans?"

"Okay."

"Who do you think? The Ashtons, of course! Stephen wields the shovel, but Marvin and Donna are in cahoots. Now, about this danger, don't spare the details. My readers deserve to know." His eyes glowed in the soft light of his face.

"Thanks for your cooperation," Tonya said. "I won't tell the Librarian you're roaming free."

"Or the Ashtons. And I want to know what you're doing about it."

"Fine, we promise not to tell on you. But we can't tell you our plans until after." Tonya looked at Priya. "Can we? Lives are at stake."

Priya nodded. "Sorry, kid."

The boy deflated. "But my exclusive!"

"You'll get it once I prove who's behind this. Do you or the other ghosts know who killed Jack Waldock?"

"Your mother Helen fits the bill."

Tonya forced a smile. "I mean the first time."

"I've heard rumors. What you need is a living witness."

"No, really?" Tonya let her sarcasm show.

"That's what's wrong with living people. No gratitude!"

"The other ghosts probably know more. It's not your fault you're little." Priya gave him a sad smile.

"I'm wise and plenty old."

"When were you born?" Priya sounded genuinely curious.

"Compared to me, you were born yesterday." The ragamuffin popped out of existence.

Tonya asked, "Can you still see him?"

"Not anymore."

"How can you see him when I can't?"

Priya shrugged. "I dunno, but I can't see the Librarian. How can you see her?"

"Old family secret." Tonya tapped the side of her nose, refusing to admit she had never seen or heard the Librarian. Her only interaction was to sign a Faustian library contract. "The ghosts know something. I'm going to the cemetery."

"Let me come, too."

"If you come, the Ashtons will assume you have your memories back. I have to go alone."

34

As she passed through the Western Gates, air shivered up Tonya's back and her feet sent mist swirling. Grass and flowers had grown back since the fall, but everywhere charred black tree stumps accused her. The cemetery was the last place she wanted to be, but Tonya needed to speak to anyone who had known her mother in high school. Maybe the Ashtons hadn't gotten to the ghosts to silence them. Tonya meandered along the smoothly paved path to the oldest section, partly out of respect, and partly to punish herself. She'd never forget.

Mostly Irish settlers had filled plots close to the once powerful Three-Century Ash. Over the decades, these Old Families had spread their ancestors up to the chapel at the top of the hill. Then, as the space filled, their descendants had progressed down to the water's edge, as if to give their departed a pleasant view.

It was a relief to see they had carted the dead trees away. Old Families had brought in sod and planted new flowers. Otherwise, offended ghosts might avenge themselves on the living. Unfortunately, gardening couldn't prevent all problems. Now and then a phantom might take umbrage at how its ancestors managed the estate. Century-old family feuds could flare up. You could read about such quarrels in *The Fading Times*.

Loon Lake Cemetery was complicated. Pures like Tonya were supposed to leave the dead in peace—or at least ignore their shenanigans. Her neglected relatives would offer no help, but Tonya hoped bored spirits from Mod or Trad families might enjoy spilling some Helen gossip. After twenty years in the ground, surely some would be eager to relive their glory days? All it would take was one chatty ghost.

Tonya left the oldest section and headed for a modern enclave where polished marble stones studded the ground. Strolling through the park-like setting, she read the dates on flat grave markers until she found the right era. When she leaned over to read an inscription, frosty air pushed her forward, nudging her into a bush. She stumbled and hopped sideways to avoid trampling someone's final resting place.

"Hello." Tonya spun to face the ghost. "Feel like a chat?" A colder gust blew back her hair, and an invisible hand shoved her chest. "Please. I'm trying to save Helen. One witness can save her."

The birds went silent. Not a cricket stirred.

"You must know something. Tell me, or Helen's death will be on your conscience." Clouds gathered overhead, and hail bounced on the grass like popcorn. She shielded her face.

"Hit a nerve, did I?" The stinging pellets grew to the size of ball bearings. "Ow! Are you trying to kill me, too?" Hail rained down the size of golf balls.

"Guess that's a yes!" Tonya covered her head and sprinted for the exit. Lightning flashed, and hail bruised her back. Chest heaving and legs burning, she sprinted out through the Western Gate.

What a transformation. Outside the cemetery, the sun warmed her face. Birds chirped against a blue sky with puffy white clouds.

"I'm sorry I burned down your trees!" she yelled back through the gates.

Silence.

As Tonya walked away, something cold and wet slammed into the back of her head. She turned around. "A snowball? That is not cool!"

An invisible child's voice snickered. "Yes, it is." Johnny appeared in her path with his old-time camera. "Watch the birdie!" The flash froze her as the shutter snapped. "Your mothers will be so proud."

35

 campus. Why wouldn't the ghosts speak to her? Did Priya's giant lizard capsize the Sea-Doo? And what did Roberto want them for?

Questions nagged her all the way back to her dorm room. After the day she'd had, all she wanted to do was throw herself on the narrow bed and close her eyes, but too many questions remained.

From a shelf in the closet, Tonya lifted down the box of library materials. Since the newspaper had combusted, she dreaded further damage, but Helen's time was running out. Giant lizards patrolled the lake. She needed info fast, even if it cost her years.

Carefully, she lifted the newspaper bundle to one side and reached for the books. It couldn't hurt to look at the covers, could it? The first item was a faded notebook decorated with band stickers and skull doodles. It was no heirloom, but she put on gloves and used an eraser-topped pencil to turn the pages.

Spidery handwriting dated the first pages to the 1980s. There was no name or signature. Entries were sporadic, dated months or years apart. The early pages were practice printing in a childish hand: A B C D RAN E. A few pages later, the author progressed to three and four-word sentences and cartoons with stick arms and giant heads. By the time Tonya found happy faces and cartoon cats, she estimated the artist looked to be in grade school.

It would take hours to work through hundreds of fragile pages, so she turned it over and worked back to front until she found 1995. The year Helen met Jack Waldock.

The crabbed handwriting switched from blue ink, to black, to pink. Curly decorations circled some words and thick lines added emphasis. In gossipy tones, the author gave teenaged girls catty nicknames. She recorded two pages of dead baby jokes and took notes from articles like "How to Kiss a Guy to Make him Fall Madly in Love with You." Finally, she mentioned Waldock:

Handsome Jack is at it again. I don't think they know he's two-timing them, but who knows? Some girls will do anything to be noticed. It's pitiful to watch them beg and plead with their eyes. Jack loves to humiliate them. That party. That girl in the bathroom. I could write it down, but nobody would believe me. It was so obvious he was stringing her along. And his best bud Lenny cackled out loud as he watched hopeful girls flock 'round Jack like moths ramming a lightbulb. Poor, confused, drunk things. They'll never understand he stands apart, sworn to love only darkness.

This continued for pages. The hateful biographer despised every female. Until the tone changed:

I don't know what to wear to the funeral. I don't have pants or a dress, only black jeans. Half the town will wear red, anyway. Ding dong, the witch is dead, as the Mundanes sing. No more envelopes of cash in the night.

The writer's soft pencil scribbles blocked out half a page, coating the paper in self-censorship. After that, the handwriting turned shaky, sharply slanted, and barely legible:

They rolled away the rock and lo, he rises again. Jack is dead, long live Jack! They'll never sell insurance in this town again. The twinkle in Len's eye is so full of joy, it glows in the dark. I'll hold on to those funeral clothes.

If only the writer had named the flock of teen girls. One was Helen, but who were the others? And who wrote the journal? Could a jealous girlfriend have murdered Waldock? A love-struck teen with untrained powers could be dangerous, especially one who liked death magic.

Tonya rubbed her jaw in frustration. She was worse off than before she started. Looked at critically, the diary pointed at Helen. Death magic? Check. Jealousy motive? Check. Hot temper? Didn't Tonya know it!

And to make her the best suspect of all, Helen's Pure family had opposed magical training—leaving their powerful daughter potentially out of control.

36

PRIYA COULDN'T LET TONYA face the graveyard alone. Since meeting the Librarian, Priya was curious to meet more ghosts. After giving Tonya a generous head start, she followed discretely. Cover was sparse until they reached the old section, where Priya could hide behind monuments.

Tonya would kill anyone who followed her, but it was clear she needed help, particularly after thunderheads gathered and a freak hailstorm drove her from the cemetery. Priya wanted to console her, but Johnny Scoop appeared in her path.

"Can you believe Tonya?"

"What did she do wrong?"

"In the newsroom, we say there's two sides to every story, but Tonya always picks the wrong one."

"Can I talk to the ghost of Jack Waldock?"

"Jack and his buddy Len have moved on, and so should you. This is no place to poke your pretty nose."

How insulting, but she made a concession for this strange old fogey in a kid's body. Priya looked him in the glowing eyes. "One of your ghost friends must know how Waldock died."

"Maybe." He took her hand and led her toward a mausoleum so old the inscription had worn away. "Show respect." He opened a wrought iron gate and dried leaves crunched underfoot as they descended into a spacious crypt.

Twenty ghosts dressed in styles from bygone eras hunched over their desks, their faces shining brightly in the glow of phantom computers. One man, in a striped shirt with rolled sleeves, wrote with a dip pen.

"This is Mr. Samuel, the editor." Johnny blushed glowing pink.

She held out her hand. "Pleased to meet you."

"Charmed." Mr. Samuel turned to Johnny. "Will she give us an exclusive?"

"Let me ask you a question," Priya said. "Do you know how Waldock died?"

"A few theories are floating in the ectoplasm." The editor chewed the back of his pen. "Normally, I ask the questions."

"Ask anything you like once you help me prove Helen's innocence."

He spat out the pen. "Helen killed Len. Saw it myself."

"But Waldock?"

"The mayor was humiliated by his son's dark magic and Len's bad influence. Some say they hired someone to make him disappear, but I don't believe that. The family told me their boy ran away, got in a car accident, and came back with brain damage."

"You don't look convinced," Priya said.

"It's a convenient way to explain his changed behavior, but I believe he died on the island. Maybe a spell backfired. Maybe his fling, Ran, fed him to a bear. Who knows? As the mayor's son, he was more entitled than rebellious. Waldock played the tough guy, but Len had a gang that tried to collect protection money."

"So, a local merchant might have killed him?" Tonya hadn't mentioned that.

"Len hadn't developed offensive powers. The owners cast protective wards and laughed at him."

"Then why did Helen kill him?"

"That's enough questions for now." He handed Johnny his pad and pencil. "Good work, Scoop. You can do the interview."

37

It would be so much easier if Tonya could just talk to Dad, but he wasn't on the scene in 1995. Mom, the logical person to ask, had blocked her number. The Pures and Trads alike were shunning Tonya, which left her to search for clues inside books that exacted a price.

Tonya set aside the precious leather-bound history tomes and chose a stack of *Fading Times* newspapers from 1995. There would be eyewitness reports and small city news. Gingerly, she untied the twine holding the stack together and scanned the first paper for mentions of Waldock's disappearance. Exactly who had been on the island when he disappeared? Was it an accident, or was he murdered for a reason?

Page-turning pencil in hand, she caressed the paper with her cotton gloves and waited for *The Fading Times* to shimmer into view. Amidst the little league sports scores and Old Family social events, she uncovered a headline that made her heart race: "Teen Necromancy."

In an interview, Len boasted he could reanimate his bestie, Jack, *if things turned fatal*. Despite rumors of teens using death magic, the editor claimed adults were overreacting. "Nobody had cheated death." Jack Waldock's supposed demise was "a teen prank," executed by Len. Police sources confirmed that Jack had run away from home several times in the previous year. They would keep an eye out but expected him to return on his own.

A stack of papers later, she read that Jack and Len had been arrested for extortion. It was their second offense, but City Council released them before the hearing when the witness recanted, and the victims dropped all charges.

Tonya flipped back through the stack. A couple of barns had burned down. Fires had leveled homes and businesses. In private conversation, Helen had called arson Waldock's signature move, but these crimes started after his death. When you put the articles and journal together, they implied Jack had become a revenant puppet dancing on Len's strings. There were investigations, but the stories petered out, perhaps to protect Mayor Waldock's reputation.

The papers were old, and the ink faded. If Tonya wasn't careful, she could exhaust the magic, obliterating evidence Helen needed for her trial. It was time to quit. She was bundling the materials when a scrap of paper slid out of the teen diary:

What is murder? Taking a life, unless it's a war. But who chooses the enemy?

She stared at the now-familiar handwriting. "What kind of kid excuses murder?"

"Goody Goody!"

"Who said that?" Tonya looked at her closed bedroom door.

"You belong in jail." The book flapped its gums or ... er ... covers.

She was being told off by a hardcover! Piggy eyes near the book's spine glared at Tonya. It shuddered and flapped its pages, pivoting on the narrow student desk to view its surroundings.

"So shabby. This squalor is not what our forefathers died for."

"My dorm offends you?"

"Worse. You reject your heritage."

"What about you? If the Staff siphoned off your magic, you'd just be a book."

"It is my duty to stamp out unauthorized magic. Give me your powers for safekeeping."

"No." She backed away from the table.

"Don't make me curse you!" It flapped furiously, expelling confetti like a dog foaming at the mouth.

Ignoring its protests, she tied it up in twine and set the book in the cardboard box. It grumbled, but the wrappings kept its mouth shut. She retied the newspaper stack and set it on top, so everything looked untouched. With the box on the student desk, she turned her back to tie her shoes.

Smoke.

Heat.

The newspapers erupted in flames that stroked the ceiling. Tonya tried to pat the fire out, burning her hands. The alarm rang and overhead sprinklers let loose cascades of spray. Swearing, Tonya grabbed her pillow and beat out the flames, reducing the papers to charred mush.

How much of Tonya's life would the Librarian extract to pay for the damage? Months? Years? Putting off the moment she found out wouldn't make things any better. She grabbed the damp box and locked her door behind her.

Chaos ruled as students clogged the hallway and stairwells. From childhood, it was drilled into Loon Lake kids to respect fire alarms. Their parents had grown up in arsenous times. It took at least ten minutes to walk down the stairs, surrounded by grumpy students.

Tonya put the damp materials in Helen's trunk and drove them to City Hall. She had to face the Librarian's wrath, but not before she asked the ghost some questions.

38

It surprised Tonya to find Priya behind the reception desk. "I'm here to return my books."

Priya's eyes popped. "What did you do to them?"

"Can you return them so the Librarian won't see? I can't afford the fines." Tonya drew a finger across her neck.

"She's a ghost, not a serial killer."

"That ghost set me a trap. The paper burst into flames, and she can demand life force to pay for the damage."

"When they dry, I'll fix them."

"It's sweet of you to try." That was how she remembered Priya, relentlessly positive.

"I can't hide from a ghost. Tell me if you see her come in."

Tonya studied her fingernails. "I can't see her, either."

"But you said"

"Sorry. I was ashamed to admit how much I stink at magic. But look at you," Tonya beamed at her friend, "in good with the Librarian, casting spells and transforming sculptures. With powers that strong, maybe you can help my birth mother. They've accused Helen of killing Jack Waldock, but he died in 1995. The cover is scorched, but it's all in the diary. His friend Len brought Waldock back from the dead, but I can't prove it, and I still don't know who killed him."

Priya lifted her nose in the air, stood ruler straight, and levitated. She pointed a finger and berated Tonya, speaking with an Irish accent. "Everybody knows your birth mother did it."

"What?" She tugged at Priya's arms, but her friend hovered firmly in place. Tonya shouted at the room. "You leave my friend alone! Get out of her!"

Priya glided to the floor and slumped over the counter. A few minutes later, she stood straight, rubbing her eyes. "I'm sorry. What were you saying? I'm sleeping standing up from welding all night. It's the strangest thing; I swear lightning is attracted to my work."

"Shh. If the mayor's office discovers you've been channeling magic, even unconsciously, they'll arrest you." Tonya looked for signs of the invisible Librarian. "Talk later." She pushed the box of books across the counter. "Please, return them discretely."

"If I don't sign them in, how will you prove they were returned on time? The late fees are deadly."

A chill breeze invaded the counter area. Priya turned to face the source. "Yes, ma'am."

From her rounded shoulders, Tonya guessed the Librarian was dressing her down. Icy wind blew back Priya's hair, sending shivers through Tonya.

The wind died, and the sign-in binder slid itself across the counter in front of Tonya.

"Any damage isn't my fault. The newspapers burst into flames by themselves. Let me speak to your boss."

"She's right here."

Tonya apologized to the empty space, but the binder snapped shut and disappeared. A second later, the books stacked themselves onto the pile of papers and floated into the back room.

"That went well." Tonya felt her cheeks heating.

"I'll plead your case later."

"Can we speak outside?" Tonya led Priya into the late June heat.

"If you can't loan me paper evidence, I'll go back to the cemetery. Maybe this time they won't pelt me with hailstones."

"The ghosts were laughing about that."

"Wait, how do you know?"

"Johnny took me to his newspaper office. It's amazing what dead folks will spill when they think you're pals."

"And?"

"Helen killed Len."

"In a wizard fight. Len and his stooges were about to kill me, so she fireballed him first. It was self-defense."

"Johnny says Helen tricked Waldock into using death magic."

"It was the other way 'round."

Priya crossed her arms. "Let's say I agree with you."

Tonya shot Priya a hard look.

"What? Helen's a badass."

"The diary says Waldock took a group of teens to the island to do forbidden magic."

"So, any teen on that trip could have killed him." Priya nodded. "That should be enough doubt to convince a jury."

"Maybe under Mundane law, but Donna summoned National Council. Reasonable doubt won't be enough when Donna influences the judge." Like during the parade. "Donna can get into people's heads and make them hear whatever she wants. It won't matter how good Helen's case is. The authorities will hear her version of the story."

"Why would Donna risk that? If she gets caught influencing the jury, the Old Families will punish her."

"Donna hates Helen."

"Enough to risk everything?"

"They're opposites. Helen has the strongest powers Loon Lake has ever seen, and Donna grew up mocked for being powerless."

"Not anymore." Priya held up a gilt-edged business card. It read: Donna Ashton, Mayor. "She's handing these out like Halloween candy."

No one could laugh at the person who controlled business permits, city security, and influenced the Old Family tribunal.

"Working at City Hall you learn a lot." Priya leaned in. "Since she came to power, her family has bought acres of protected city land."

"From squatters to landlords."

Tonya could never clear her mother in the court of public opinion. National Council would hear the Ashtons' arguments and find Helen guilty.

The tang of fish increased as the wind rose, sweeping across town. Citizens swept front porches with extra vigor, and children played tag like rugby players, grabbing each other too hard and yelling too loud. Frenetic energy rippled through every living thing, but from what source?

Deep underground, insects twittered in their burrows, agitated by a subsonic bellowing too low for human ears. Hungry leviathans scraped across the sand and slipped into the depths of Loon Lake to hunt.

Flocks of gulls dispersed, and ducks abandoned the waves.

No loons.

No cormorants.

Not a single water bird remained.

39

WHEN HER PARENTS SPLIT up, Dad leased a condo in Toronto and saved Tonya a bedroom. Mom took a one-bedroom apartment on the fringes of Loon Lake City, close to fellow Pures. She then stopped talking to Helen and Dad.

Twice during the drive, Tonya had thought about turning back. Mom would never support Helen. Expecting Mom to turn her away, Tonya buzzed from the lobby. When she stepped out of the elevator, Mom was waiting in front of her door clasping chafed hands. Neither spoke until Mom closed the door behind them.

No kiss. No hug. Mom pointed Tonya into a living room chair and went to bustle in the kitchen.

Tonya raised her voice to be heard in the next room. "Helen's been charged with murdering Jack Waldock."

Mom spoke through the pass-through. "Don't let her drag you down."

Tonya went to the kitchen doorway. "She's your sister."

"I can love the criminal and hate the crime."

"Donna wants National to execute her, and with the Staff of Storms, she can use Helen's powers of persuasion to rig the trial."

"If Helen's innocent, there's nothing to worry about." Mom opened a canister. "Coffee?"

"You were around in '95. Who wanted to kill him?"

Lips compressed, Mom stared at the wall, letting water overflow the carafe.

"If I can't find another suspect, Helen's only hope is to get elected mayor and pardon herself."

Her mother laughed bitterly while still facing the wall. "Nobody will vote for her."

"What if you ran? You have sway with Pures and Trads."

Mom scoffed.

"You don't think you can win?"

"If by some miraculous chance I did, Helen would still have to face National Council."

"You wouldn't pardon your own sister?"

She left the carafe in the sink and faced Tonya. "This has to be our last visit."

Pure protocol dictated that mom shun Helen and Tonya—come flood or zombie apocalypse. This would be Tonya's last chance to ask.

"Helen went to the island with Len and Jack when they were teens. What do you know about it?"

Mom covered her mouth with hands marred with eczema, the nails bitten to the quick. In the months since her breakup, Mom looked older. "I couldn't join that crowd, obviously—and besides, Jack ran away from home and came back."

"You believe that?"

Mom shrugged. "When I was young, people didn't go around raising the dead." She walked to the door and waited for Tonya to leave.

"Giant lizards have attacked swimmers at the beach."

"Helen charms animals. We're safer with her in jail." Mom held the door open.

"Please help, for my sake." Tonya tried to hug Mom, but she flinched away. When emotion didn't work, Tonya appealed to her mother's beliefs. "Donna will abolish the laws against using magic."

"Have faith. People will never vote for an Ashton."

<h1 style="text-align:center">40</h1>

As an unincorporated municipality, the Mundane side of Loon Lake depended on the Provincial Police for security. Locals called the tiny local detachment on Main Street the Cop Shop. Left over from when it was a record store, the storefront had a plate glass window, which Tonya used as a mirror to finger-comb her snowy locks into respectability.

Inside, a counter divided the tiny waiting area from the workspace beyond. At her approach, the constable working the desk glanced up from his smart phone and frowned. His name tag read Tilson.

Tonya steadied her voice. This would take finesse. Without mentioning Drake or Priya, what could she say to trigger an investigation? "I found something dangerous at the beach. Let me show you?"

"What?" Dark circles shaded his youthful eyes.

"I felt magic from the riverbank, near the studio on campus."

"Tonya Fitzpatrick." Yawning, he lifted the receiver. "Your parole officer should know you've been sensing magic."

"I can't help what I sense." She reached over and covered the dial pad. "Swimmers disappeared from the public beach. I found huge, clawed footprints in the sand."

"Thank you, Nancy Drew. You don't need the police." He leaned across the counter until Tonya saw veins in his bloodshot eyes. "You need to learn your place."

"A giant lizard is loose on the university campus."

"Okay, you've convinced me. I'll send a car." He returned to playing with his phone.

"When?"

"Now. Absolutely." He didn't look up.

"And you're going to check it out?"

"The R.C.M.P. should arrive in under five minutes." He stood and turned his back to straighten a picture frame.

"Tourists disappear and you cover it up?" She struggled to keep her voice down.

"I'm too busy to waste time on Bigfoot prints. You can't use magic. Your real Mom is in jail, and your adopted one rejected you. It's okay to ask for help, but I'm not your therapist."

"Giant lizards could eat people."

He came around the desk and towered over her. "You're hallucinating from unauthorized magic use. That's a reportable crime."

"Are you threatening me?"

"Marvin tells me that kind of investigation drags on, but they hold the accused in the meantime in the interest of public safety."

Either the Ashtons had paid him off or blackmailed him—probably both.

It looked like the bad old days were back.

THE PUBLIC BEACH BUZZED with activity as carefree folk celebrated summer, ignorant of the danger. A group of teens played volleyball on the golden sand, and the whole town, from tots to grannies, frolicked in the sun. It was impossible to find Shin in such a crowd, until Tonya noticed a familiar stroke cutting through the water.

There was no time to admire Shin's technique. Scanning the water for people-eating lizards, she waded into the shallows and waved him ashore.

His smile faded. "What's wrong?"

"The Ninjas are filming on the island, but they aren't answering texts or calls. Let's talk in private."

Tonya led Shin behind the boat rental, stopping between the canoe and kayak racks. "People have disappeared from this beach, but nobody in authority cares." She described finding the beach scattered with towels and abandoned valuables.

"Relax. Police said some kid threw up in the water, so they closed the beach."

If he saw something, the Ashtons had already wiped his memory. "Loan me a boat? The Ninjas are in danger from giant swimming lizards."

He laughed.

Tonya put her hands on his shoulders. "Think back. Do you have any blanks in your memory? Sensations of déjà vu, particularly around Halloween?"

He raised an eyebrow. "How did you know?"

"I need that boat."

"If the boss finds out, he'll fire me." Shin reached on the rack for a canoe.

"Give me a fast boat. These creatures are hungry."

"We could search together." He gave her a concerned look. "Can you dive?"

"Sure, but I'd rather stay on top of the water."

"Bring cash, and I'll rent us a twenty-footer. There's extra SCUBA stuff in the team locker. I have to see these giant lizards."

"Bring harpoons."

He stopped grinning when she said, "The biggest you have."

Shin stepped out of an electric car. "When did you learn to dive?"

"Grade eleven," but high school felt like another lifetime to Tonya.

He opened the hatchback. "I got us the best tanks and regulators."

Tonya pulled off her t-shirt, sweats, and sandals, leaving them in the car. Her feet burning on the hot asphalt, she hauled a diving belt around her waist and fastened it. Facing each other, they slipped on their tanks and checked each other's equipment with their masks propped on their foreheads. It was the first time Shin had seen her in a bikini, but he kept his eyes on the job.

Swim fins in hand, they tiptoed across the lot, crossed the sand, and finished on the pier overlooking the lake.

"Sure you know what you're doing?" Shin asked.

"Not my first rodeo." She hoped that sounded cool, but she didn't need to impress Shin. He acted friendlier, and he'd lost some swagger since she first met him. A side-effect of the memory wipe? "You don't have to come." What good was saving the Ninjas if a monster swallowed Shin?

He scoffed. "I only agreed to this because I wanted a dive buddy for the cave. Also, you have a boating license, right?"

"I thought you rented the boat in your name?"

"About that. We're sort of borrowing it." Shin played with his mask strap. "If the police stop us, flash them your license."

"But I paid you cash for the rental!"

He shrugged. "When the boss is away…" He stepped into the boat and held out his hand.

Shin's arrogance was intact after all.

She stepped onto the hull and took the keys from Shin. It was the first time she'd driven a boat with a steering wheel and an inboard motor. She pumped the choke button to get the gas flowing and turned the key. With a rumble, it started on the third try. When she pushed the accelerator lever, the boat roared away from the pier.

Shin high-fived Tonya. "Next time I bring water skis."

The boat thumped rhythmically as they sailed over the waves.

"Whoa, Captain. You're a beast!"

She shrugged. Magical creatures sometimes sensed magic, and something had attacked the Sea-Doo. Did it home-in on her powers?

"Put on your regulator!" she shouted over the engine noise. If they capsized, he'd be able to breathe.

"Relax, we're still close to shore."

They were headed for the island, but the creatures could be anywhere, fishing or fighting, or doing whatever else giant lizards did. Tonya hoped if they attacked the boat, she wouldn't instinctively fight back with magic. What if Donna's curse kicked in while Tonya was deep under water?

42

WHEN THEY GOT CLOSE, Tonya eased back the throttle and circumnavigated the island. The Ninjas had left their boat tied up to the pier, but after a complete circuit, she hadn't spotted them. The island was miles long, and Betty's wards blocked her phone.

It was hot, even with the breeze, and Shin unzipped his wetsuit to the waist. "Where do we look first?"

"Keep your flippers on. If I know Zain, he'll be filming in that creepy underwater cave."

They idled into the cove closest to the tunnel, and Tonya anchored offshore. She slipped on her fins. "Ready?"

They sped through their pre-dive checks and rehearsed hand signals. It was their first plunge together. Sitting on opposite gunnels of the boat, they signaled thumbs-up, then tipped in backward.

Underwater, Tonya kicked ahead of Shin. He might captain the diving team, but Tonya was a water baby. Flippers made her want to somersault and splash like a dolphin.

Coming alongside her, Shin gave her the thumbs up. Good, he was paying attention. On the way down, Tonya glanced at his broad shoulders and muscled torso. With a sigh, she took a long pull from her respirator and exhaled a trail of bubbles. It made her feel guilty to put such innocent perfection in jeopardy, but what choice did she have?

Fifty feet from shore, the lake bottom was a smooth rock face, fuzzed with five o'clock algae. Visibility was good, except for where deep voids punctured the lakebed. Were they new? Local waters lacked sunken wrecks or colorful fish, so a deep hole would have attracted notice. Tonya pointed Shin toward a massive breach in the lakebed, so new the edges were clean.

They raced for it, Shin surging ahead like an orca shot from a cannon. Well ahead, he reached the dip, stirring up muck that hid him from view. Tonya hovered over the deep space before she glimpsed his retreating flippers disappear.

Before she could follow, Shin shot back up, eyes wide inside his face mask. Underwater, a damped, strangled scream reached her as he shot past before Tonya could get turned around. Heart pounding, her legs pumped as she raced to the silvery surface.

A water wall slammed into her. She spiraled ... sideways? The murky dark obscured direction. Letting her body go limp, it took ages for buoyancy to tug her upward, but that was all she needed to orient herself. In a burst of kicks, she broke the surface, seeking Shin or whatever had spooked him.

Whitewater! The torrent slammed and tossed her like clothes in a washing machine, and the current dragged her down.

Her hands scraped rock. Tonya peered into the murky darkness. Her headlamp revealed an algae-filled tunnel where the calm water made her feel weightless.

Ahead, her light reflected off something shaded by murk. It was as big as her face, an antique gold dome with a dark round center. There were no treasures in Loon Lake. What had formed that perfect circle? Something familiar tugged at her memory. What was she missing?

The formation blinked.

A giant eyeball! She froze, then kicked onto her back and oh-so-gently fluttered away. Had the leviathan noticed her? Probably. Unless it slept with its eyes open.

Water churned and surged beneath her. Tonya sprinted for the mouth of the shaft. The creature's grasping lips tickled the ends of her flippers. She strained for every bit of acceleration.

The thing opened its mouth and created an undertow that tugged her backward.

Kick harder.

Harder.

But she couldn't get away. A long, pink tendril snaked around her waist and squeezed until her stomach ejected acid into her respirator. Wriggle and kick all she might, the tongue squeezed her stomach until she couldn't breathe and made her air tank creak under pressure. The silvery surface faded as she started to black out. What a stupid way to die. From her belt, she released the emergency float, so they could find her body.

The beast retracted its long elastic tongue, pulling her foot into its jaws. With a snap, it sliced through a flipper.

Think. Think or die. She had no weapons, no harpoon or knife.

She grabbed a diving weight off her belt and used it to hack at the long slender tongue that was wrapped around her waist. But the plastic-coated weight bounced off. Tonya spit out her regulator, held her breath in her throat, and opened her mouth. She bit into the tongue and started to gnaw.

Subsonic cries shuddered through the lakebed. The beast shook its head, tossing Tonya left and right, but she closed her jaw tighter and wouldn't let go until it clamped shut.

She had sheared through!

Bellowing, the creature retreated, sending Tonya reeling in its backwash.

Replacing her regulator, Tonya inhaled deeply. Air was sweeter than chocolate, hotter than Drake, and much better than death. She fled upward before the creature could get over its shock.

She surfaced near her floating emergency signal, which Shin had nearly reached, and she sprinted toward the approaching boat.

"Hurry!" Shin screamed.

A dome of bubbles rose beside her as the monster returned for revenge.

43

An enormous wave rose, and she rode the momentum to the side of the boat and hauled herself aboard. She lay with her back against the bare aluminum hull, panting at the sky.

"Head home." She heaved a breath. "Fast."

A thin aluminum shell floated between Tonya and the thing's jaws. Reaching with her mind, she detected blips of life force radiating off tiny fish and bigger ones. A vast cluster of energy directly below the hull resolved into two.

"There are two lizards."

Pushing Shin aside, she grabbed the wheel and slammed the accelerator, heading for the cove.

Shin swore. "Why'd you bump me?"

"To save your life."

The smaller creature had multiple life signatures fluttering inside. One monster was pregnant, and she was hunting with her mate.

44

ONCE THEY REACHED SHALLOW water, Tonya turned off the engine and let the boat drift up to a small beach. She hopped out, and Shin threw her the rope tied to the prow. Together, they dragged the boat up onto the sand until Tonya figured the lizards couldn't see it.

There was no path from there, so they pushed their way inland through the brush to where the granite bulge rose out of the greenery. When they reached the rungs drilled into the rock, she said, "We have to climb to the top. There's a split in the rock above the cave where the Ninjas do their filming."

"I've got no shoes to climb with." He flexed. "Fortunately, I'm a god."

She followed Shin, thankful she'd brought surf shoes in the boat. Maybe she would never love heights, but she had proven she could do it. Her first few steps up the ladder were easy, but she reached halfway, and her legs stopped. The treetops below her looked too small. The smart move was to back down the ladder and leave it to Shin, but Drake was in danger. No time for self-indulgent plummeting to death. Tonya forced herself to look up and moved her feet and hands slowly, without another stop.

At the top, she crawled over the edge and kneeled close to the split in the granite. It was too dark to see the bottom. "Drake! Grace!"

Shin joined her. "Zain!"

The wind blew softly, rustling the pine trees.

Weird. The granite egg sounded like it was breathing. Quietly, she backed away.

Shin sauntered to the far side of the rock, arms spread to his domain. "I am legend!"

"They aren't answering. Let's go in."

He waved her off as a keening song filled the air. The otherworldly crooning soothed her fear of heights and worries about the Ninjas. "Do you hear that?"

"What?"

It was a lullaby, a siren song, an irresistible invitation to join it in the cavern. Tonya clapped her hands over her ears. "Don't let me go down there."

"What if the Ninjas are inside?"

The ethereal song drew her to the cave. "You're right. I have to go in." Her voice came out syrup slow, her tongue too thick for her mouth. "Can't you hear it?"

Shin shook his head.

"Too bad." To hear it was ecstasy.

45

MOLD ON THE ROCK faces tickled her nostrils. On a twenty-foot ladder, she should have shivered with fear, but every rung filled Tonya with a loving warmth that evaporated any anxiety. Her feet touched stone, and she led Shin into an immense cavern lit by the Ninjas' halogen lamps. A row of earthen mounds blocked her view of the subterranean beach. The nearest stood taller than her.

"Zain! Drake!" Shin stopped. "The Ninjas must have built these hills for their film."

"Keep going toward the singing."

Shin planted his feet. "Hello? Anybody here?"

No reply.

"This feels wrong." Shin turned back. "I say we leave."

"You'll miss the interesting part." She took Shin's hand and led him to a stonier part of the cave where mounds rose ten feet from the mucky floor. "Look."

In a relaxed heap lay a school bus-sized lizard with a long tail. Smiling, Tonya watched the pouch under its jaws inflate with each breath. Slate-blue scales cast a rainbow sheen that contrasted with its pale belly.

Leaving Shin to gape, Tonya kneeled in front of this perfect creature, wishing it would open its golden eyes so she could lose herself in its gaze.

Shin swore. "All I have is a diving knife," he whispered. "How do I stop that?"

"We aren't fighting."

"Damn right. We should run!"

"No, its partner needs food for their babies."

"Huh?"

"Stop and listen."

She grabbed him around the arms. He struggled until his face went slack, and she knew he heard it, too. Shiny-eyed, Shin followed Tonya to a big mound of sand.

Celestial crooning filled Tonya until her heart wanted to burst for joy. It felt so right to sacrifice herself to Mother Lizard's beautiful children.

"What are you waiting for? Start digging."

"Hello?" shouted a deep voice from within the mound. Was that Drake trapped inside? Anybody but him!

"Help us!" Her boyfriend's voice broke the enchantment.

"Forgive me." She slapped the back of Shin's head.

"Ow!"

"Shh. Pretend you're under the spell. If the mother lizard thinks she's controlling us, she won't attack."

"I thought you were trying to walk me into her jaws."

"Sorry about that, too." She edged over to a mound. "Start digging. She expects us to bury ourselves."

"When we asphyxiate, will that be part of your plan?" he asked. "We have to free these people."

"Mother Lizard is watching, and these mounds are her baby food, so start digging."

The scaley creature heaved itself to its feet and stared until Tonya showed Shin how to paw at the sand in a dreamlike cadence. Tonya whispered, "Once they leave, we'll wake the others and climb up the ladder."

"When you heard the song, why didn't you tell me to leave?"

"It gets in your head and makes you want to sacrifice yourself."

"What?"

"I'm not sure I can resist."

"Don't worry. If you try to get me killed again, I look forward to slapping you."

Tonya dug until her fingernails snapped off. Her hands bled from abrasion. The whole time, she felt Mother Lizard's huge golden eyes on their backs. When Tonya slowed to wipe sweat off her brow, the enormous reptile nudged her leg.

"Okay, I'm digging." She dug slower while she strategized. Could she break through the mounds without attracting notice? What if her friends were suffocating?

At long last, Mother Lizard dozed, and she left her mound to check on another. She scooped a hole near the top with bloody fingers while, nearby, Shin dug into a different mound.

"It's hollow inside." He moved to let Tonya see.

Shoulders, arms, hair. Bodies clustered in a pile.

"Are they alive?"

"They're breathing." Shin burrowed like a dog after a gopher.

It was the same in her mound. Several bodies wearing swimsuits, still breathing.

"Wake them up," Shin said. "Let's go."

Tonya uncovered a hand manicured in gold, Grace's signature color. Reaching in, she patted her sleeping friend's cheek.

Grace didn't stir, so Tonya pinched her arm hard. No reaction. "Wake up!"

Shin joined Tonya, and they grabbed Grace around the waist. The unconscious girl's arms dangled over their shoulders as they heaved her out, but they couldn't carry deadweight up the ladder.

"Wake up!" With a sandy hand, Tonya tapped Grace's cheek.

Oops. A large golden eye peered over the mound at them. Mother Lizard was awake.

46

Encased in sand and wrapped in a cocoon of angelic sound, Tonya let Mother's tender care caress her from the ears out. It filled her with joy to watch Shin's eyes droop to the song. Mother Lizard dug an unconscious woman from a nearby mound. She used her claw like a scalpel to cut a line down Marta's belly.

Surely that was wrong? Mother Lizard loved her sleeping treasures.

Panic mounted in Tonya's throat. Shouldn't she help Marta? Tonya trembled, her mind clear enough to understand this was an emergency, but her arms and legs wouldn't move.

Then, the song reasserted itself and lulled Tonya into peacefulness. She could only watch sleepily, unable to control her reactions. There was something she desperately wanted to do.

Oh, yeah. Now she remembered. She wanted to stay with Mother.

Mother Lizard expelled an egg from her mouth and pressed it into the gash in Marta's stomach. Tonya tried to scream, but she couldn't open her mouth. Her limbs weighed hundreds of pounds. The nightmare had her paralyzed, but that's all it was. This was a dream. It wasn't real. Satisfied, she settled back to sleep.

Why had she ever worried?

Hours later, pain awoke Tonya, directing her to look at her stomach. Something had torn the front of her shirt away. A puckered scar ran up her belly in a jagged line. Pain raged, but her hand came away blood free. What magic was this?

A phone flashlight switched on, and she saw Shin beside her, trapped in the same cramped airspace. He looked unharmed but covered in sand.

"I have good news and bad." His voice was raw.

"Okay."

"The good news is we're still alive because the mound has air holes."

She pointed to her belly. "This is the bad news."

"That and two giant lizards are waiting to eat us."

"If we stay, a hungry creature will hatch and eat me from the inside."

"What?"

"I saw Mother Lizard plant an egg inside Marta, too."

He dug feverishly, but Tonya put a hand on his shoulder. "Wait. Save your phone battery until they leave."

"How will you know?"

"I feel their life force."

"How many people have they trapped inside these mounds?"

Through the pain, Tonya closed her eyes and let her senses reach out to tiny points of green light surrounding them. "I feel the life force of fifteen people, but some are fading."

"If they're too weak to climb the ladder, the lizards will catch us."

"Mother Lizard won't hurt me." She felt for Shin's wrist and placed it on her abdomen just as something turned a victory cartwheel inside its shell.

Shin took her in his arms. "I'm so sorry." His kiss warmed the top of her head. "Don't worry. Someone will come for us."

"Why wait? All we have to do is dig ourselves out, get past two people-eating hypnotic lizards, sneak to the back of the cavern, and climb a thirty-foot ladder in the dark with unconscious people on our backs."

He chuckled. "Piece of cake, until Godzilla sings you a lullaby and you fall off the ladder."

47

Tonya held her breath. By the light of Shin's phone, they crept toward the back of the cave, keeping the dirt mound between themselves and the sleeping lizards as much as they could.

Sand crunched underfoot. Shin was moving too quickly. Tonya whispered, "Point the light down. You'll wake them." Ahead, the ladder stood in a slash of daylight.

"Couldn't we wait until they leave?"

"I lost blood when Mother Lizard cut me open, and my head's spinning."

"I'll come back for you."

"Unless she sings you back to sleep."

Shin squared his shoulders and crept forward. Behind Tonya, the leviathans spluttered as if rousing out of sleep. Her stomach heaved with nausea, and the pain made her lightheaded. There was no way she should lead when she might fall off the ladder.

"I'll keep watch. Go. Now." With a grunt, Tonya bent over her bulging belly and picked up a rock. It wasn't much of a weapon, but it felt better than empty hands.

Halfway up the ladder, Shin waved for her to follow. The first few steps were easy, but as the ground receded, her hands shook. Too much blood loss added to her fear of heights. *Don't look down. Deep breaths. You can do this. You will not pass out.* Forcing herself to smile, because it helped prevent her from throwing up, she took the next step and the next.

It worked, too. They were going to make it!

Mother Lizard's crystalline notes pierced the air, sending Tonya right back into her musical cocoon.

Arms and legs fused to the ladder, and Tonya clung in place, swooning. The cold hard cave suddenly filled with sweet, warm air. Mother would make everything better.

"What are you doing?" Shin backed down the ladder and held out his hand. "Come on, Tonya."

Shin was so silly. Couldn't he hear? Tonya closed her eyes and let her head fall back. This was bliss, made even better when Mother Lizard nosed up underneath her. One touch and she felt safe. All she had to do was lie back on Mother's snout and let her return Tonya to the nest. Home.

Pain seared through her hand.

"Ow!" Shin had stomped on it.

"What are you doing?" She could just kill him! Or kiss him? Mother's serenade confused everything.

He grabbed her hand, and the bones in her wrist popped. He dragged her up the ladder, the pain in her wrist melting the cotton candy filling Tonya's head until she was fully conscious and scared.

Clarity lasted until the pain faded, and Mother Lizard's lullaby overwhelmed her with bliss.

"You go. I'm staying with Mother Lizard." Tonya leaned her head back, letting her hair fall into space as she swayed with the music. Love and safety were right below. Mother would make it right. She just needed to let go.

A slap across the face woke her.

Whoa! Tonya shook her head. What was she thinking? She grabbed the rock out of her pocket, twisted to face Mother Lizard, and took aim. They were so close. The beast could wrench Tonya off the ladder with its teeth. Tonya launched the rock into the reptile's eye, then raced up the ladder.

Mother Lizard's bellows shook the granite walls, dislodging dust and mold.

As they scrambled out of the crevice, the deep thundering of her mate answered. The creatures couldn't squeeze through the shaft, could they?

"Run for the boat!"

Ahead of her, Shin clambered down to ground level as cedar trees and bushes burst into flames, stinging Tonya's eyes with smoke.

Shin coughed. "It came out of the water. How are we supposed to reach the boat?"

"Gimme something to stuff my ears."

He gestured at the nearby trees. "Take as many flaming leaves as you like."

Tonya ripped a strip from the bottom of her t-shirt to make earplugs. If they could get to the water before flames engulfed the island, they might survive.

Dead ahead, Father Lizard opened his maw, claws planted to withstand the backward propulsion of the fiery blast he aimed at Shin.

Tonya yanked him behind a boulder in time to miss the blast. They retreated into the trees, but the beast was panther quick. In moments, it would pounce. There was no escape and no way to outrun it. Shin was going to die, and it would be her fault.

"I'm going to stay here and stall. It won't kill the person carrying its egg. Go. Take the boat. Get help."

"But—"

Tonya took a step toward the angry beast, palms-up and smiling. "Chill out, Big Guy. Be nice to your surrogate mother."

48

THE MONSTER RUSHED AT her, and Tonya backed away slowly. "Come on, Papa. Be nice."

Its mouth twitched. Would it flame her? She froze. Like an angry bull, it roared and thrust its head left and right, snuffling to home in on her scent. The good thing about Father Lizard was he didn't sing. The bad thing was, he didn't seem to care about the egg she carried. Tail switching across the ashy ground, the creature advanced, made eye contact, and braced its legs.

Oh no.

It thrust its mouth open, and Tonya dove behind a tree. Flames burned the ground and stung her feet before the blast sent her cartwheeling onto her butt.

Tonya held still.

So did the beast.

She peeked at the bottom of her blistered feet. The dragon turned and headed for the shore ... and Shin.

No. Shin had to get away.

"Hey, you call yourself a father?" She stood shaking a fist until it turned on her.

The beast bellowed as it chased Tonya, who sprinted and dodged, weaving in and out of the bushes. Father Lizard flamed left and right, charring Tonya's shirt, and reducing lush bushes to flaming wooden skeletons.

The leviathan was gaining on her. She needed a proper hiding place.

"Ow!" Her blistered feet stung with every step as she sprinted for Betty's invisible staircase. But all pain disappeared when she smelled the beast's carrion breath at her shoulder.

Now, to find an invisible staircase. There was no time to concentrate and sense for magic. Tonya found the area where she'd seen Betty's property, but only found a shack. *Betty's illusion had better work on giant lizards.*

Using the shack as a landmark, she explored until her foot struck something, tumbling her forward. The invisible steps! She went by feel. Kick, step, kick, step.

Once she grabbed the railing, Tonya bounded to the top without looking. The second her feet touched the deck, magic shimmered, and a wide wraparound deck came into view. Tonya stood, panting. The front of the house was pine and glass in chalet style, with a pitched tin roof. Pretty sweet compared to the shack that was visible.

Betty's illusion disguised her majestic house from people, but could it hide Tonya from a magically enhanced monster?

The metallic click of a safety catch made Tonya turn. Betty trained a rifle on Tonya's face. Tonya put her hands up, then pointed down the hill.

"Dragon ..."

Betty lowered her gun. Smoke and flames tore through the forest canopy. Betty's eyes widened as Father Lizard thrashed through the undergrowth to stand on the beach below.

Tonya's heart pounded. "Can it see us here?"

"We'd better go in before it smells you."

Betty led Tonya into her chalet. The mud room held rubber boots, a rack of tools, and a rifle rack hanging over the door to the living room. Betty did not put the rifle away before she signaled for Tonya to go ahead.

They passed into a high-ceilinged living space. One wall sported a weathered plow, and a glass washboard. Pot lights glowed from an antique wagon wheel hanging from the ceiling. Luminous oil paintings of barns with cows, fields of wildflowers, and Loon Lake's Main Street graced barn board-covered walls. Betty had good taste.

"Sit." Betty pointed to a couch facing the deck and the lake beyond. "I'm trying to decide whether to let the dragons have you."

"You could have warned me about them before."

"Shh. They can't see us in the house, but they hear very well."

Tonya whispered, "Why stay on the island if dragons can eat you?"

"They're new, and I have bigger problems. Who knows you're here?"

"Please." Tonya pointed at her slashed belly. "The mother dragon put an egg inside me."

"Disgusting." Helen went to the kitchen.

Tonya followed. "There are fifteen more like me in the cave. If you don't help, when the eggs hatch, they'll die."

"I can't do anything."

"You could shoot the dragons."

"Might as well shoot myself." Betty reached for Tonya's belly but pulled away. "Tea?" She propped the rifle beside the stove.

"There's no cell service. Can I use your landline?"

"I don't have one." She left the tea things and sat facing Tonya. "Before you contact the outside world, we need to talk."

"The island's on fire, and I don't know if my friend Shin got away." Tonya stood. "And there are dragons on the island!"

Betty filled a battered kettle, then strolled to the living room window. "It's starting to drizzle. Rain will put the fire out."

Tonya pointed to a long, dark form in the lake. "If I'm fast, I can rescue the swimmers while Father Lizard is hunting."

Betty blocked her path to the door. "First, we need to talk."

"Okay." What had Tonya read about hostage situations? If you got to know your captors, they were less likely to shoot you. "Where did you get your beautiful oil paintings?"

"Acrylics. Did them myself."

"Incredible. How can you paint Main Street so perfectly if you never leave the island?"

"I lived there many years ago."

"Why paint a place you don't like?"

"The place is wonderful. It's the people I can't stand."

Tonya forced a chuckle. "You sound like me. I wanted to study in Toronto, where they wouldn't remember me as the picked-on kid."

Betty gazed at her paintings. "Sometimes I dream I'm back in Loon Lake."

"So return. Or move somewhere else."

"Ashton Security would make me disappear." Betty's jaw clenched.

"I hear you. Since they let me out of jail, a ghost follows me everywhere accusing me of murder. At first, I thought the cemetery ghosts made him do it. They know Helen and I settled Waldock in October."

"Killed him."

"No, we settled a revenant and saved the town."

"Agree to disagree."

Tonya remembered the hail incident. "I fixed the ghost, too."

Betty leaned in. "How?"

"I tricked him into admitting the truth. If he didn't spy on me, Stephen Ashton was going to dig up his grave."

Betty swore. "Thugs."

"You aren't surprised?"

Betty nodded, as if encouraging herself to speak. "I returned to Loon Lake once, but ghosts surrounded me at the dock. They threatened to spy on me and make my death look like an accident. The worst thing is, I'm innocent."

"So testify. We can get Helen out of jail and find out who killed Jack Waldock together."

"Nobody stands against the Ashtons. You should move to the island with me." Her lips twitched in a smile.

"Please. National Council will sentence her to death. You were with Jack the day he disappeared. Who else was there? What do you remember?"

Betty stared at the wall long enough to memorize its atomic structure. Finally, she met Tonya's eyes. "Maybe Helen acted for the right reasons, but I can't testify. Or go back to the mainland. Donna would ..."

Tonya touched her belly. "If nobody opposes her, things will get worse."

"I'm so sorry."

Tonya scanned the water but couldn't spot Shin's boat. *Maybe he made it.*

A portrait above the fireplace caught Tonya's attention. Painted in glowing oils, the young man's expression was proud but stern, lit from within against a background of stars.

"You painted Waldock!"

Betty came back, gun in hand.

"It's beautiful. When did you do it?" Tonya asked.

Betty returned the rifle to its holder in the mud room. "I don't remember. All I do is paint."

The artist had exaggerated his handsome features to create Jack Waldock, teen icon, bathed in celestial light.

"You loved him."

"Don't be silly." Betty blushed.

"You can't return to Loon Lake because the ghosts accuse you of murdering him. You love him, or you wouldn't hang this on the wall. What else are you hiding from me?"

"I loved the real Jack Waldock." She stroked the portrait's cheek. "Before he became Len's puppet."

"So, you killed him in 1995?"

"It would have been a mercy, but no."

"If you loved him, demand justice. You're imprisoned on this island while the real murderer goes free."

49

Betty wouldn't testify or leave the island, but Tonya couldn't give up. The recluse had been there, and Tonya was sure she was involved in Waldock's death. If the witness wouldn't talk, Tonya had to search for clues.

"Can I use your facilities?"

Betty pointed to a narrow hallway lined with doors. The first was the master bedroom. The second was the bathroom. Tonya went in and turned on the faucet. A quick peek assured her Betty wasn't watching, so Tonya dashed to the third room.

"Ow!" Tonya's head struck an invisible barrier hard as a block of ice. She stumbled back and almost walked into Betty who glared at her, hands on her hips.

"Get out!"

"Sorry, I was curious."

But Betty didn't relent until Tonya stepped onto the deck. She descended the stairs until her view of the window was blocked by trees, and then she waited. The third room barrier was just like the one Miranda had used to block Helen's jail cell. Could Betty cast the same spell? Sometimes magical abilities ran in families. Were Betty and Miranda related? Or had Miranda set the ward?

Tonya stood still, listening for Father Lizard, but heard only chickadees and sparrows sheltering from the gentle rain which extinguished the fires. The beast was probably in the lake, catching fish.

Alert, but seeing no sign of danger, her mind returned to essential questions. Where exactly had they murdered Jack Waldock? Twenty years later, DNA evidence would have eroded, but spell traces and ghosts lingered for many years. As she crept through the bushes, she wondered why Johnny hadn't floated onto the island to harass her. Was he afraid of the giant lizards? Unlikely. They couldn't hurt him. Did the island repel ghosts? Had someone banished Johnny?

Tonya returned to the deck and circled around to the back of the house where there were steps down to Betty's garden. The lawn fell away in wide terraces. On the top terrace, at the end farthest from the house, she recognized the pond with its fairy lights in front of the enormous half geode.

Betty defended her domain with a rifle as if she was hiding something, and this magical space was a good place to look for it. Behind the amethyst geode, rocks framed a garden lined with cedar chips. The flowers looked healthy and well-watered. Tonya identified chrysanthemums, a rosebush, sweet William, and rosemary. According to plant lore Helen taught her at the shop, rosemary was for remembrance. Roses were for passion, and chrysanthemums stood for loyalty and love.

The hair prickled on the back of her neck. Symbolic flowers hinted at a memorial. Her conviction increased when she found a cairn of stones beside the garden. Betty could have gathered rocks to keep animals out of a compost heap, but there weren't any potato peelings.

Tonya was sketchy on how necromancy worked, but if they brought Waldock back from the dead, didn't that mean the corpse got reanimated and there was no body to bury? Was this garden a memorial to Waldock or someone else?

Reaching out with her mind, she detected tingles of power nearby. It could be plant life or traces of a faded spell. In a nearby tool shed, she found a long-handled spade and started digging. It was agonizing. Her hands were raw from digging sand, and her feet were burned and blistered. Every time she stepped on the spade, it hurt, but her body had gone into emergency mode. She didn't feel thirst, or hunger, or even the incredible fatigue she should feel by now. Whenever Tonya stopped to catch her breath, her fingers stung, but when she thought of Helen, the spade felt lighter, and she dug with vigor.

The sun had set by the time she tunneled under the pile of rocks. Muscles aching, she declared it empty. If they buried anything, it had returned to the soil without a trace. Her efforts had earned her nothing but new blisters. Exhausted, she threw down the spade and sat on the cairn of rocks.

Cold.

So unnaturally cold, it chilled her legs through. She spread her palm against the stone, and it chilled her fingers until they ached. Dark images filled her mind, a hurricane of despair. The rocks were mourning, a memory of dread soaked into their core.

No doubt. Waldock had died here, and this wide, flat rock would never forget it. Betty's painting and this shrine meant she was an innocent bystander who loved and cherished Waldock's memory. Otherwise, she was the sickest kind of murderer who kept souvenirs—and belonged in exile.

Cool breezes brushed her cheek. By the light of her phone, she picked her way down through the trees, slipping on mud and stones until the earth flattened out.

Time to find a hiding spot where she could wait for the supply boat. Thankful for the moonlight, she headed around the coast, looking for the public pier. As she went, she kept one eye on the water for hungry lizards.

Where was Shin? He was supposed to bring help. She held up her phone. Still no signal. It looked like Betty's wards kept out ghosts and cell phones.

Around a corner, she spotted the pier, a winged lizard crouched on its wooden slats. Had it seen her? Tonya backed away slowly.

Her foot snapped a branch. The lizard opened its golden eyes and charged. On instinct, she leaped into the nearest tree and scrambled up. It wasn't until she had climbed halfway to the top that she regretted her error.

The beast let loose a stream of fiery breath.

Flaming leaves surrounded her while the beast waited for her to drop into its hungry mouth. Its reptilian grin widened. Was she nothing to this dragon but a marshmallow on a stick? She worked her way out onto a branch and thrust out her belly.

"See this? This is your egg, buddy!"

Flames ignited the branch she stood on. *So much for fatherhood*. She considered leaping from this tree to the next, but she wasn't a monkey. And even if she could jump that far, the monster would burn down the next tree and the next.

Tonya closed her eyes, concentrating on the pulsing life forces around her. In her mind, the tree glowed as its natural energies streamed forth from its trunk like a halo.

The beast reached for the lowest branch. It shimmied up quickly. A claw reached up, and the next one would grasp her.

Sorry, Miranda. Let's hope whatever's blocking ghosts and cell phones also blocks ankle monitor signals.

Tonya latched onto the life energy of the giant lizard and let it fill her with vitality. No longer winded, Tonya drew its power faster in a race to weaken the beast before it closed its grip around her.

Roaring, it fell off the branch. With a head shake, it charged the tree trunk like a rhinoceros. The tree shuddered, and Tonya clung hard to the waving branch. The lizard circled and attacked, battering the trunk until the wood cracked. Concentration broken, the energy link between them failed, and the branch under her snapped, sending Tonya tumbling.

Tonya leaped to her feet, but it was too late. The dragon was upon her. She threw out her hands as they collided.

Like lightning, contact reestablished the connection. Drawing energy body-to-body, the flow quadrupled. It reminded her of the battle with Waldock, except this time she wouldn't have Helen to haul her off the body before she joined it in death.

Could she break the connection on her own?

Too late to turn back. If she stopped draining energy, it would come to its senses and roast her alive. But she was feeling giddy with the excess power. Too much more of this and she would lose control.

Wishing there was some other way, Tonya redirected the beast's life force into the earth, shaking the ground underfoot. It thrashed its tail, bashing a nearby tree, but doing no damage. She had to stop before she killed it. Tonya sidled up to the creature to check on it.

It seemed weak until it turned and clubbed her head with its tail.

50

Fluorescent lights flickered overhead. On the hospital bed, Waldock's body manifested. With a nod from Helen urging her on, Tonya grasped his slimy hand and braced herself to siphon his life force.

Power! She floated to the ceiling, bubbling up in a never-ending river of joy.

Until his energy turned dark and painful, sending flames of sand through her veins. Waldock was taking her down with him! If she didn't break contact, she would die, but her cement limbs refused to move.

Paralyzed and hyperventilating, Tonya awoke.

Mist obscured the moon as waves rolled onto the pebbled shore. The shadowy heap of the dragon lay limp beside her. She had survived without Helen's help. Dragging heavy feet, she stood to check the sky and lake. The male lizard's dying cries must have carried halfway across the lake. Its mate would leave the nest to investigate, which gave her a chance to rescue the swimmers.

Tonya rushed through the bush until she reached the stone mound. There would be no second chances, so Tonya found the footholds on the smooth granite face and climbed to the top. In the dark, fear of heights bothered her less. Or maybe it was the adrenaline. She soon stood at the top, scanning earth and sky for the dragon.

Roars and splashes sounded in the distance. A back fin cut through the water, and Mother Lizard's great tail switched as she circled the island, cruising toward the pier where her mate had died.

Tonya clamped hands and feet onto the sides of the ladder and let herself slide, firefighter-style, to the cave floor. She ran to the sand mounds, kicking them apart and urging, "Wake up! Wake up!"

Bodies stirred, and women and children stumbled out of their sandy prisons.

"We have minutes before the dragon comes back. Help wake the others."

Some victims stumbled about in a daze. Others dug into mounds with their hands, constantly checking for dragons over their shoulders.

Tonya unearthed Zain. "Hurry, or Mother will catch us."

"Mother ..." Zain grinned sleepily settling back against the sand mound.

"I see why you like her, Zain. She can breathe fire, rip down a tree, and swallow you in three bites."

That cleared his head. "Grace! Grace!" Zain ran in circles, kicking sand in every direction. "We were watching the rushes when a dragon started singing to us."

"What about Drake?" Tonya's chest felt like it would burst.

"He's here somewhere." Zain smoothed the sandy tip off another mound, releasing four gray-haired men in swim trunks—and Drake!

Tonya rushed over to brush the sand out of his eyes and off his face.

"Tonya?"

When he stepped away from the mound, relief flooded through her. She put her hands on either side of his face and kissed his sandy lips.

When he came to his senses, his eyes dropped to her distended belly. "What happened?"

"It's a curse. No time to explain." She redoubled her efforts until they found the last mound near the back of the cave. Zain and Tonya dug frantically until they found Grace buried upright with Marta. Tonya didn't understand how that was possible. How could Donna Ashton's daughter be caught like the others?

"This way!" Drake urged the stragglers up the ladder.

Most climbed awkwardly, encumbered by the unfamiliar weight of their rounded bellies.

When the line dwindled down to two, Drake tried not to stare at her stomach when he said, "After you."

Tonya gritted her teeth and climbed, despite her fear of heights and her awkward new center of balance.

Drake emerged from the gap. "Are you going to tell me what this is about now?" He pointed to her abdomen. "Everybody looks pregnant." They stood together until the last person got out.

"I might have a solution for that, but I'm too weak to try it."

Now all she had to do was keep the others safe from Mother Lizard, so she wouldn't sniff them out and eat them while they waited for the supply boat.

51

WHEN THE LAST SWIMMER stood safely on the ground, Tonya was dreaming on her feet. Between micro-naps, she noticed Marta kept to the back of the group and wouldn't make eye contact, her hands supporting a watermelon belly.

"Can't the dragon see us in the dark?" Grace searched the bushes with her phone light.

Zain rocked on his toes. "It's probably curled up in its cave. Monsters need their ugly sleep."

"They were sleeping in their cave during daytime," Tonya said. "They could be nocturnal."

"Like mini fire-breathing vampire Godzillas." Zain's eyes gleamed.

"Idiot." Marta chided more gently than usual.

"Shouldn't you be scared?" Grace asked.

"I'm only scared you'll kill the last one before I get it on camera. With actual monsters, who needs CGI?"

"Don't worry. We're going to the ultimate hiding place." Tonya gathered the survivors and led them to the base of Betty's staircase. "Promise not to tell anyone about this."

Revealing a magically hidden staircase to Mundanes broke every Old Family rule, but it was the only safe option. "I'm going to disappear by going up an invisible staircase. Watch." She thumped loudly up and down several steps so they could hear what she did.

"Ready? Find your way with your feet. There's a handrail, too."

Marta went first. As she passed Tonya, she said, "Mom's going to hear about this."

Zain zipped up the stairs so fast you'd think he could see them. Drake followed, but it took longer to convince the others it wasn't a trick or a trap.

Zain was already knocking when Tonya reached the deck.

"Give up, Zain. She hates people."

"Maybe she's deaf." He kicked the bottom of the door.

"She hears perfectly and carries a rifle."

This deflated him until he looked over the balcony. "What a view." Zain pulled a DSLR from under his jacket and nudged Drake. "Let the dragon come! I want to record it in flight."

"You don't." Tonya pointed to scorched trees and patches of ash. "It could roast us and incinerate the deck. It can't see us." She faced the group huddled on the deck. "We'll be safe here as long as we stay quiet."

Marta had mysteriously left the group, which shuffled and whispered. A thin mother rested her hands on a toddler's shoulders. "My kid's hungry. Let's see what's in the kitchen."

"Betty will shoot if you try."

Speaking softly, Grace took the woman by the arm and led her to the far end of the deck.

Objections rippled through the group. These people were traumatized and deserved to be treated with decency. It was stupid of Betty to refuse them hospitality, but Tonya didn't trust her not to shoot. She checked the time on her phone.

"The supply boat comes in six hours. Take a drink in the garden and then try to sleep. I'll stay awake and watch for the dragon."

Drake put his jacket around her shoulders. "Let me take the first watch. You look ready to fall down."

"I'm fine."

The deck was too hard to sleep on, but she could sit and rest. Using Drake's jacket as a pillow, Tonya propped herself against the wall of the house and closed her eyes.

52

RAINDROPS SPATTERED TONYA'S FACE.

"You shouldn't have let me fall asleep." Tonya struggled to sit. It was exhausting whenever she drew life force.

Drake opened his arms and Tonya melted into his warmth, letting his strength buoy her. When they broke apart, Tonya gazed into the pale sky. "How long till 8:00?"

"A few more hours."

"Good. Let the people sleep some more before we go to the pier."

"Whatever shall we do while we wait?" Drake teased a hair away from her face.

A white sky met the silvery smooth surface of Loon Lake. Tonya's stomach growled as the supply boat cruised into view, a tub toy moving at rubber ducky speed. At least, that's how it felt to Tonya as she checked the sky every two minutes, worried Mother Lizard would pick off survivors before help arrived.

With agonizing slowness, the tub toy resolved into a little barge. The captain, a skinny rag doll with long gray hair, tied up at the dock. Paying them no attention, she rolled a cart onto the pier stacked with flats of groceries.

How could she walk past the survivors in their ripped clothing? She had to notice their sand-stained faces and the ones with protruding bellies.

Tonya and the Ninjas converged on the captain. Her tiny eyes, sunken in an apple doll face, squinted up at Tonya. "What are you doing here?"

"A giant lizard wants to eat us." Tonya kept her tone calm and rational.

"Is that all?" The captain tried to drive the dolly past.

Tonya stopped it with her foot. "Please take us back to Loon Lake."

"No."

Zain slipped behind the lady while Drake shot her a confident smile. "How much should we tip you for the ride?"

"I'm not a taxi."

"We're stranded," he said.

The captain pursed her lips. "Phone someone with a boat."

"You must know phones don't work here." The Ashtons had gotten to this woman like so many others. "Look at that mother and her little daughter. They're tired and hungry, and your boat is big enough to take us all."

"I can't." As the woman stared at Tonya's round belly, Zain reached into her pocket.

"Gimme my keys!"

Zain dodged around the groceries and ran for the bushes.

The captain sprinted after him, skirting trees and rocks, but Grace caught up to her easily with long strides.

The captain was gaining on Zain, and was about to snatch back her keys, when he skidded to a stop and faced her.

"Mwah, ha, ha ha!" He grinned and popped the keys into his mouth.

"Ugh! You are disgusting." The woman stood, arms akimbo.

Grace stifled a laugh. "We'll give them back," Grace placated the old woman. "Let me help you carry the groceries first?"

The woman narrowed her eyes. "Since I have no choice, you push the dolly."

The woman returned to the boat and gathered an armful of loose bags, then strode inland, followed by Grace with the dolly.

Tonya knew better than to tag along after bringing all these people to the recluse's door. One look at Tonya, and Betty might shoot her head off.

"I'll help." Drake hurried after them.

"Who knew thieves were so helpful?" The woman glared back at Zain.

"I've always wanted to drive a boat. Plus, I can radio for help."

"You know how to do that?"

He shrugged. "How hard can it be?"

Huddled for warmth, the survivors shivered in damp clothes. Several women wore bloody t-shirts that were ripped down the front. "We can go home soon. Is everyone okay?"

Children emerged from the bushes clamoring around Tonya.

"I'm hungry."

"When's breakfast?"

"I want Daddy."

They followed her to the boat, which had a sunken deck. "We'll be safe on shore soon."

She stepped in first and gave each person her hand to steady them over the gunnel. Once they settled in, filling most of the space, she asked. "Did you hear Mother Dragon singing?"

Woman, child, and man, they all nodded.

Zain called back from the helm. "There's no radio. What do you want me to do?"

"Get the engine running. We leave as soon as Grace and Drake get back."

Once the engine started rumbling, Tonya approached a youngish blonde with an obvious rip in her t-shirt. "I'm Tonya. What's your name?"

"Lea."

"Lea, can I look at your wound?"

The woman shook her head and gestured at her teen daughter nearby.

"Please." Tonya led her into the head for privacy. She seated the woman on the bathroom counter facing away from the mirror. "Are you okay?"

"It hurts, but I can walk."

"I think I can help. May I?" Tonya pulled Lea's shredded cotton shirt aside. A vertical slash divided Lea's belly, jagged and purple like a month-old scar.

"How did this happen to you?"

"We were at the beach building sandcastles when I heard a wonderful song coming from the water. The next thing I knew, I had climbed onto one of the giant lizards. They swam to the island, swishing their tails back and forth." She sniffed. "How could I bring my kid?"

Tonya steadied the woman's shoulder. "It wasn't your fault. Can you tell me any more?"

"We got off at the island, hypnotized by that tinkling music. Everything felt wonderful until the monsters scooped up this lady and dove under the water. I tried to run, but each time the lizards sang, my legs walked me back. We lay down in their mouths, and they bound us with their long, rough tongues." The woman shuddered and spit on the sand. "It's like I can still feel their saliva on me."

A ripple of movement crossed Lea's belly. She tried to hide it.

"I'm so sorry, but it cut your belly and put its egg inside. It healed the wound with magic, or you'd have bled to death."

"No." Lea covered the bump with her hands.

"Magic can be difficult to accept."

Lea was about to go, so Tonya lifted her tattered shirt. "They got me, too."

Lea's voice quavered. "What happens when they hatch?"

"I can prevent it." Tonya reached out.

"Don't touch me!" Lea ran to her daughter and tried to hug her.

"Mom! Not here." When Lea didn't let go, the teen's embarrassment changed to concern. "Are you okay?"

"Yeah."

Until a parasite started eating her mother. Tonya couldn't stand by and watch that happen. "I think I can sterilize the egg."

Lea hesitated.

"Let me try." Tonya hoped she was strong enough.

The woman let Tonya lay hands on her belly.

Tonya had to isolate the woman's life force, otherwise she might kill Lea at the same time. She closed her eyes and concentrated on the faint glow of life inside the shell. There was power there, but when she tried to drain it, nothing happened. The prison anklet didn't heat, and she couldn't channel energy. Not one spark.

Something on this boat was blocking her magic.

53

Once Tonya stepped onto the dock at Loon Lake Beach, her powers hummed back to life. The boat had been charmed to suppress her powers, but now she could act.

"Lea, help me gather everyone with belly scars."

The affected individuals encircled Tonya except for Marta, who hung back.

The others watched as Tonya lay hands on Lea's scarred belly. Eyes closed, she drew the life force out of the egg as hard as she could. Dizzy, she swayed with fatigue, but she had to finish before she got caught. The woman's life depended on it.

As the last dregs drained out of the egg, Tonya's ankle monitor burned her skin.

"Am I cured?" Lea glanced at her daughter.

"I'd see a doctor about your wound, but the egg is gone."

"Thank you!" Lea hugged Tonya, almost toppling her to the boards.

Marta pushed ahead of the afflicted beach swimmers who crowded around, each wanting to be healed next. Exhaustion mounted as Tonya helped person after person until she had drained the last spark of life from the survivor's parasites.

After the others rushed away to meet their loved ones, Drake looked at her belly. "What about you?"

"I'll need to recover first, but I can cure it."

He whispered in her ear, "You're incredible." He put his arms around her shoulders.

"So are you, but no hugging in public. Donna would love an excuse to fry your brains."

In a just world, the whole town would cheer them for rescuing the swimmers. But this wasn't a just world.

Mounting pain scorched Tonya's leg, raising a circle of welts. She looked across the beach to the parking lot just as Miranda stepped out of an Ashton Security van. Flanked by two meaty armed guards, Miranda quick-marched across the parking lot.

Before she could arrive at the beach, Tonya whispered to Drake, "You aren't supposed to know me. Go."

At the foot of the pier, her parole officer grinned. "Couldn't resist, could you?"

Miranda signaled for Tonya to turn, then cranked on handcuffs. With the guards flanking them, Miranda paraded Tonya to the van.

Drake loitered at the edge of the parking lot, staring. If he tried to help, Ashton Security would learn the memory wipe had failed. Hands bound behind her, Tonya silently implored him to leave.

It was hard to watch him fight against his protective instincts, but eventually, he turned away. Had Miranda noticed?

"You have a date with the Staff of Storms." She shoved Tonya forward.

"Dragons attacked us." Tonya twisted against her bonds to look back at Miranda, who seemed unsurprised to hear about dragons. How many people were in on the secret?

"Move it."

"They took people from the beach and buried them alive. I had to rescue them."

"The law is the law. Motive doesn't matter." Guards ordered Tonya into the van, chained her to the bench, and shut the doors, plunging her into darkness.

54

WHEN THE VAN DOORS opened, Tonya squinted at the sunny lawn in front of City Hall.

"Take a minute. Catch your breath." Miranda took her place behind Tonya.

"Aren't we going to see City Council?"

"We have to make a stop first."

Miranda eased Tonya toward a parking lot behind the building. A crowd had gathered in front of a raised platform. Red and white bunting decorated the railings, fastened with maple leaf rosettes. This had to be for Donna.

A sweaty, musclebound guard took over for Miranda. "Up the stairs. Let's give everybody a good look."

"I can't climb with my legs tethered."

"Move it, princess. Your public awaits."

Before she could take three steps, Johnny shimmered into view and shoved a phantom microphone into her face.

"You hid on the island to break parole. How does it feel to get caught?"

"I'm proud of defending the town against a monster." Tonya took halting steps up the stairs, leg irons jangling with each movement.

"That's it?" Johnny flew in front of Tonya again. "Gimme an actual quote."

"I'll save it for the voters." If Donna intended to parade Tonya in front of the public, they deserved a good show.

"Better say it quick, then. Donna pressured City Council to move up the election to tomorrow!"

"How?"

"The same way she is influencing the voters—with Helen's powers. The Staff of Storms sure comes in handy, and now you've played into the Ashtons' hands. They're about to capture your power, too! What do you say about that?" He paused, pencil in hand, poised to record her quote.

"Why won't you print the truth? The Ashtons are corrupt, and Donna's election means disaster for Loon Lake. They knew dragons snatched people off the beach but didn't do anything."

He trailed her up the stairs, moving to the opposite corner when the guard escorted Tonya to the back of the platform. From there, Tonya had an excellent angle on Donna, ready to address the crowd.

Dressed in another red skirt suit, her hair eerily still despite the breeze, Donna stepped to the mic stand. "As your representative, I will show mercy to those who fail out of weakness. But in the name of justice, willful offenders must be punished."

Despite the early hour, the audience applauded loudly. Firefly news drones sparkled with magic as they rose to platform level, sending a live feed to the Old Family News.

Donna pranced in front of her supporters, blathering about limiting magic, civic pride, and job security. At least Tonya was out of the spotlight until the beefy guard trapped Tonya's arms against her sides and pushed her to the railing.

Donna greeted her supporters with a sunny smile. "Good people, look at this young criminal. I'm sure you recognize Tonya Jones, daughter of Helen Lennox. Much to her shame." A pregnant pause gave listeners time to cluck. "Tonya refuses to control herself. She snuck off to the island to use magic, breaking her parole." Donna tut-tutted. "But she isn't as smart as she thinks she is."

Some individuals heckled. Another cheered, "Donna for mayor!"

"It pains me to say Tonya's birth mother is a Pure, in name at least. If Helen Lennox becomes mayor, she will enforce an anti-magic policy on every citizen—except herself and her wayward daughter." Donna pointed a blood-red nail at Tonya. "Helen denied Tonya for eighteen years, an even bigger hypocrite than her child. She's in jail for murdering Jack Waldock. Helen doesn't want to serve you. She only wants to be mayor to pardon herself." Donna raised her pitch. "Well, pardon me!"

The audience chuckled.

"As a volunteer and then a counselor, I have dedicated my life to serving Loon Lake. Can I count on your support?" Donna flexed raised arms in triumph as the crowd chanted, "Donna! Donna! Donna!"

When the hubbub settled, she adopted a serious tone.

"To protect Loon Lake, I promised that if this dangerous prisoner broke parole by using magic, I would take away her powers." She held out a hand, and a campaign organizer handed her a polished hardwood staff topped with an enormous amethyst.

Brandishing the Staff of Storms, she ordered, "Observe and bear witness!" Donna pounded the staff on the platform three times.

In the blue sky, thunderheads gathered over Donna's head. With a crackle and roar, lightning flashed near Tonya in a storm no wider than the platform. A weight shifted inside the egg. Tonya had worn herself out by curing the other swimmers, and Miranda had arrested her before she could help herself. Once Donna stole her powers, Tonya would be helpless to stop the parasite from growing inside her belly.

Despite her fatigue, Tonya focused on the egg inside, straining to detect its tiny life force and neutralize it in time.

Thunder cracked as radiant plasma snaked between Tonya and the staff, pulsing with energy. As Donna's spell leached away her magic, Tonya lost focus and wobbled on her tethered legs. For Helen's sake, she kept her chin up and refused to look weak. Donna's supporters would love to take a clip of her kneeling in defeat and make it go viral.

The guard nudged Tonya's legs from behind. Nobody would've noticed, but it toppled Tonya onto her hands and knees. Jelly-legged, Tonya tried to rise, but Donna's hand on her shoulder held her down. The guard poked her back with his stun gun as a warning.

Blowing the crowd kisses, Donna gloated. "Justice. That is the Mod promise. To serve justice, we must defeat Helen!"

The crowd roared as they led Tonya away.

55

THE GUARDS RELEASED TONYA behind the platform. Just as well. Tonya didn't want to be followed as she stumbled away, trembling from the aftereffects of losing her powers. At least there was no reason to imprison her. Stripped of her abilities, the Ashtons couldn't claim she posed a risk to the public. They were the ones poised to do damage. National Council would arrive the following afternoon.

The first thing Tonya did was call Shin to make sure he got home safely. Next, she returned to campus for a shower, a meal, and a change of clothes before driving to Helen's store. Using Helen's key ring, Tonya let herself into the shop and through the door to the private staircase.

It felt strange standing in Helen's home by herself. Odd smells wafted from the neglected kitchen, but there was no time for housework.

Helen would need a suit and decent shoes for the trial. On the second floor, Tonya found the master bedroom and a walk-in closet. It had been so long since Tonya spent time with Helen that she didn't know her favorite outfits. Tonya walked her fingers from hanger to hanger.

The red jacket? No, that was Donna's color. The black? Not if she wanted to look innocent. Tonya chose a pale blue dress and navy shoes. Crisp and clean.

It was hard not to speed on the drive to see Helen.

It felt weird to hand over her phone and purse to Miranda and sign for them, almost like Tonya was a prisoner again. She stood with her hands at her sides, clutching the dry-cleaning hanger a bit too tightly as she waited to be let in.

If seeing her walking free disappointed Miranda, she didn't show it. She simply initialed each item and wrote her signature with a flourish underneath. Something bothered Tonya about that, but she couldn't quite grasp it.

In her cell, Helen looked smaller, her white hair limp and dull with grease. Tonya lifted the dry-cleaning bag and shoes. "I hope these are okay."

"Perfect."

When Tonya tried to pass them through the bars, an invisible barrier stopped her hand. Behind her, Miranda snickered. "No gifts for the prisoners."

"It's a suit to wear at the trial. Can you give them to her?"

"No, and your visit is up in ten. The Losing Candidate needs time to practice her concession speech for tomorrow."

As the guard retreated to lean against a wall, Tonya noticed a flash of silver below Miranda's pant leg. On a hunch, Tonya lunged at her ankle and felt it through the cloth.

Tonya awoke on the floor, drooling, her arms and legs paralyzed. She tried to say *You zapped me!* But it came out, "Youzzz!"

Tonya twitched with aftershocks but smiled through her drool. Miranda was wearing an ankle monitor, too.

"Are you okay?" Helen shouted through the invisible partition.

"I'm fine. It's a misunderstanding." She struggled to move her limbs but couldn't stop grinning. Miranda lived in the catacombs under City Hall, the only guard who did. She never left jail, bullied people like an inmate, and wore an ankle monitor. Didn't that make her a prisoner?

"Can you get up?" Miranda frowned down at Tonya.

"The floor's so nice and cool." Also, her legs were all jelly.

Miranda had never stood trial. As an employee of Ashton Security, her unusual treatment made Tonya think her punishment came from Donna Ashton herself.

Flopping onto her side, she questioned Helen. "The night Waldock died on the island, who was with you?"

"I wasn't there."

"Yes, you were." Stun gun in hand, Miranda gestured at Helen.

"I was on the island," Helen said. "It's not the same thing."

"Selective memory." Miranda pointed the wand at Tonya. "Get up unless you want another blast."

Tonya remembered where she'd seen the same handwriting as the journal—the prison logbook when she signed over her purse. "You're Ran. You wrote the diary."

Helen's voice rose. "What did you do?"

"Wouldn't you like to know?" Miranda asked.

"Twenty years later, and you still bicker like girls." That gave them pause. "Ran is locked up with you. Betty is imprisoned on the island. Does Donna think all three of you murdered Waldock?"

"She loves punishing people," said Helen.

"I dare you to move out of prison," Tonya told Miranda. "If nobody's making you wear that ankle monitor, you can leave."

Tonya sank back on the floor. She had to catch the killer before Helen ran out of time, right after she regained use of her legs.

56

On wobbly legs, Tonya stumbled into the sunlight. She propped her back against City Hall and texted Priya.

Working?

—yes

Bring me the journal I borrowed. I can prove H innocent

—k

Her limbs still trembling from the shock, Tonya let herself slide down the wall and sat to wait. Evidence in the journal would convince Betty to testify, but not coming from Tonya. Her white hair and family traits reminded Betty of her hated rival, Helen.

Tonya felt strong again by the time Drake drove up with Zain.

"Show this to Betty. It proves she and Helen were both innocent. I didn't understand what I was looking at before, but Betty will."

When she handed the journal to Drake, Zain tried to snatch it away.

"Don't damage it!" She glared at Zain. "The Librarian will hurt Priya." Tonya explained the fine system in Loon Lake.

Tonya touched the side of Drake's chiseled jaw and drew them together, forehead to forehead. She needed his help but hated putting him in danger. "Betty might listen to you."

Drake took Tonya's hands in his. "I'll bring Grace. When we delivered the food, she and Betty clicked."

57

THE NEXT DAY, TONYA went to the beach to support her mother. As Donna's sole opponent, Helen had been released from prison long enough to make a concession speech.

A throng already crowded the sand when Tonya arrived. On the rooftop patio of the boat rental, Marta and the Ashton brothers flanked Donna, ready to celebrate their victory. Kids played with balloon animals, and the sweet smell of cotton candy mixed with popcorn to enhance the carnival atmosphere. Across the front railing, red-and-white bunting gleamed in the sun. Cameras flashed and journalists raised mics to capture Donna's first words.

Meanwhile, invisible to Mundanes, firefly cameras darted and hovered, sending live images to the Old Family Newsfeed.

Tonya smiled at Drake, Zain, and Shin, and her heart swelled. Defeating the Ashtons was nearly impossible, but she wouldn't be fighting alone. Her best friend, Priya, was onside, and so was Grace.

"Everybody ready?"

"Don't worry," Priya said. "We'll text you as soon as we see Helen."

Drake and Zain melted into the crowd while Tonya and Shin guided Betty toward the boat rental. It was a gamble, but she was determined to show Loon Lakers a new side of their new mayor.

When Donna stepped to the mic, the crowd hushed. "I'm grateful for your overwhelming support." Donna lowered her eyes and batted phony lashes with fake humility. When she placed a manicured hand on her jaw and opened her crimson lips in a show of surprise, Tonya scoffed. How could anyone believe Donna's act?

"I want each of you to know how much it means that you have entrusted Loon Lake to me and my family." Donna raised her arms in triumph. "We will do our best for this beautiful city."

It surprised Tonya when Donna didn't send magical sparks into the crowd. When she gave her parade speech, Donna had magically reached into the minds of each voter to detect and deliver what they wanted to hear. This afternoon, each citizen heard the same words.

Why the sudden honesty?

Moving slowly, Tonya led Shin through the excited crowd around the side of the boat rental so they could go in the back door and upstairs to the rooftop.

Amplified to rock concert levels, Donna boomed, "Nightly patrols will keep Mundanes out of the Old Village section of Loon Lake."

A ripple of surprise went through the crowd. Since when did residents vote for a militia?

Two Ashton security guards flanked the back door to the boat rental. The assault rifles in their hands gave Tonya a shiver, but she approached politely.

"Gentlemen, Donna asked Betty to speak next."

"Why aren't you in custody?" asked a huge guard built like a plastic action figure.

"The charges against me were dropped. I'm innocent."

"Whatever." A chuckle sent ripples through his bulging biceps. "Get outta here."

"There's been a misunderstanding. Let me at least speak to Stephan Ashton?"

"Yeah, right. Now go."

On the stairs behind him, Marta and her Mod besties chuckled.

The action figure's partner was thinner, with ropey muscles. "Don't make us subdue you." He flexed his hand over a stun gun holster.

"Sorry, my mistake."

Tonya backed away. With a nod, she motioned for Shin to slip through the crowd with her. They stopped under a tree that overhung the back corner of the roof.

"Can you give me a boost?"

Shin made a stirrup with his strong fingers. "I'm right behind you."

"If we can't get Betty in by the direct route, I'm going to distract the guards. Tell Drake it's up to him."

The rough pine bark covered her soft hands in sap. She had chosen this tree for height and because the branches grew straight out of the trunk like spokes. She put her hands on a higher branch, heaved herself up, and swung a leg onto the branch to stand. Progress was sweaty. Slivers stung her hands and sap dripped on her head. At least she'd smell piney fresh.

Once she reached rooftop level, she waved down at the guards in full view of the crowd.

Action Figure Man and Ropey Arms left their post to shout at her, "Get out of the tree!"

"I want a good view."

"Come down!"

"Okay. I'll try." She looked at the ground and quivered, grabbing the tree trunk and holding tight. "I'm stuck. Get me a ladder?" It was easy to act panicky, drawing on her recent experiences.

Action Man left, leaving his ropey-armed companion to guard the bottom of the tree. Tonya texted Drake: *Go!*

Below and in front of her perch in the tree, Donna's eldest brother, Stephen, took the mic. For the occasion, he had taken the pencil off his ear and put on a sports jacket.

"Donna disappointed our parents. Imagine, a Mod child born with no powers."

A big-bellied supporter jeered, "Idjit. Don't insult Donna!"

"I wish they could see this moment." He put his big hands on Donna's padded shoulders.

"Little Donna has made us proud. Her policies put the hard-working Old Families of Loon Lake first. Thanks to her, your children will develop their magical talents and grow up in prosperity. It's time to claw back our ancestors' power and regain space to grow in our fine city. Thank you, little sister, for never giving up."

Marvin chipped in over Stephen's shoulder. "Way to go, little sis! Never let the Trads keep you down!"

From her vantage, Tonya saw Shin leading Betty alongside the boat rental.

"I'm falling!" Tonya screamed, bringing Ropey Arms and Action Figure running. From her perch, hanging upside down from her knees, Tonya saw Shin escort Betty onto the rooftop.

Blood pooled in Tonya's head, making it hard to watch Shin slip in front of Stephen and grab the mic. "This is Betty. She doesn't choose to live on the island. The Ashtons imprisoned her there. Tell them."

Tonya swung onto the branch and sat. A handful of Ashton Security Guards on the rooftop converged on Shin, who grabbed the wireless mic and tossed it to Drake. He handed it to Betty, urging her to the front of the balcony.

Betty stared at the crowd. Before she could speak, a guard broke away from Shin and tried to grab her. Drake leaped into his path. Ouch. Drake landed on his back with the guard on top, tussling.

Another guard sidestepped Shin, headed for Betty. Before he could grab her, Zain clambered over the railing and jumped on his head, wrapping skinny arms and legs around his neck.

"You're killing me!" Zain shrieked. "Put me down!"

This got a laugh, but the audience quieted when Betty spoke into the mic. "For many years, I told myself I didn't care what happened to Loon Lake. But this week I've met a new generation that deserves to live free." She stared into the crowd, looking a bit lost until Grace shouted and gave her the thumbs up.

Betty pulled the mic out of the stand and paced as she spoke. "I was there, twenty years ago, when they murdered Jack Waldock. Helen didn't kill him."

Donna's supporters booed, but they couldn't drown out Betty's calm words. The guards held Zain, Drake, and Shin with stun guns to their backs, but Betty, the legendary recluse, commanded attention.

"It's not murder to settle an undead monster."

A journalist shouted into a megaphone, "Who did it?"

"Not Helen."

"Then why is she on trial?"

"Donna followed Jack everywhere, blinded by puppy love. She was a kid, but we were teens. Jack wasn't interested, but that didn't cool Donna's obsession. When she grew up, she avenged herself on Helen. That's why she put Helen in prison. Donna imprisoned me on the island because she thought I was part of a conspiracy to kill him. Every time I tried to escape, a league of ghosts met me at the dock, and the Ashton Brothers threatened my life. And for what? I didn't murder Jack Waldock. I loved him."

Donna tried to grab the mic. "People kill for love."

"Then maybe you did it." Betty turned on Donna. "Jack went out with Miranda until Helen came along. Helen's ability to channel power excited him so much that he forgot everyone else."

"Necromancy!" Donna sneered.

"Was it? Helen, Ran, and Len gathered at the flat rocks that night. Miranda was expecting Jack to propose. She'd been hinting all summer. Delusional child. Normally, Jack flitted from girl-to-girl, but when the full moon rose, he proposed to Helen."

"Delusion is a terrible thing." Donna put on a concerned look and put an arm around Betty. "We're on your side. No need to make a fool of yourself."

Betty brushed Donna away. "Ran lost it, said if she couldn't have Jack, nobody could. When Jack started casting a spell, she came from behind and shoved him. He fell headfirst, hit his forehead on a boulder, and it killed him."

The guard holding Zain released him and fled down the stairs, followed by Zain shouting, "Wait up!"

"Please excuse her ravings." Donna beamed a plastic smile.

"I saw it." Betty kept her eyes on the crowd.

"If you knew who did it, why didn't you tell the police?" Donna threw her hands up like a terrible actor.

"We panicked. We were kids. Miranda told us our evil magic made her do it, and we were all responsible." Betty pointed at Donna. "You kept the secret, too."

"How?" a journalist shouted through a bullhorn.

"Jack's father was mayor. Dying while doing death magic was a scandal, so they covered it up."

"Don't listen to her." Donna's face turned red as her lapels.

"The murder released masses of power, but Len captured it for himself." She paused. "I've often suspected it was Len's influence that turned everything sour. He didn't have a lot of magic on his own, but everywhere he went, disagreements erupted and friends turned on each other."

"These lies would be funny if they weren't so pathetic." Donna chuckled. "Jack Waldock came home."

"Len reanimated Jack as a pliant zombie," Betty said. "That gave Len control over Waldock's powers and preserved Mayor Waldock's reputation. When Helen's hair turned white, it proved she'd used death magic. The Old Families rejected her, so she left town. Miranda and I went back to school. We thought all was forgotten until Donna became a councilor. Under Donna's influence, the Ashtons built a magic-proof prison and came after us."

"Why?" asked a journalist.

"We excluded her because she was younger and had no powers. Donna wasn't invited that night on the island, and she never let us forget it. To her it didn't matter which of us killed Jack. She wanted to avenge herself against all of us."

Donna tried to slap Betty, who grabbed her wrist and kept speaking. "She thirsted for revenge, but we were too powerful to attack directly."

From the tree, Tonya shouted, "That's why Miranda lives in jail wearing an ankle monitor. Donna put her away for life without trial!"

"Just like me." Betty slumped. "If I came back to Loon Lake, the Ashtons threatened to kill me."

"This poor, crazed woman has been living alone too long." Donna smiled. "I can arrange a proper facility with medical help." Donna tried to put an arm around Betty.

She stepped away. "You'd like that. Everybody under your control."

Tonya backed along a branch until she was over the roof. She dropped to the patio and stood beside Betty so she could speak into the mic. "Your prison uses the Staff of Storms to redirect people's abilities. You needed Helen in jail, so you could use her persuasion to con the electorate."

Donna headed for the stairs, but a guard blocked her path. A pair of guards held Drake and Shin, but the others hung on Tonya's words. Finally, her message was getting through.

"During this campaign, no matter what you said, voters heard the promises they hoped for!" Tonya shouted. "You used my ability to absorb power and boosted Helen's ability to sway voters. The election is a fraud."

A handful of guards thundered up the stairs and carried Betty away. Before they could get her too, Tonya leaped for the nearest branch and climbed back into the pine tree. Once she was out of range, Tonya shivered, thinking of what Donna might do to Betty if their plan failed.

"That was ... interesting," Donna addressed the crowd, twirling an index finger beside her head. She coughed "crazy" into her hand.

Supporters chuckled, but the crowd roiled with shouting and arguments.

"Now, I want to unveil the cornerstone of our plan to revitalize the Old Village of Loon Lake. Signor and Signora Alvarez, come say a few words."

From her vantage in the tree, Tonya watched two short people and one tall come out of a green-and-black pavilion on the beach. They strolled along the waterline, letting the crowd wait. Roberto strutted, and his parents, so modest in stature, swaggered like their son.

When the Alvarez couple took the mic, Donna seemed to shrink into a chair upstage.

A flutter of applause greeted Signora Alvarez. "Loon Lake stands on the world's biggest reserve of magic. We will prosper when we share it."

Roberto towered over his parents. "Mundane sympathizers beware."

He snapped his fingers, and the pavilion's sides dropped away, revealing a giant lizard lazing on the sand. Roused by the shouts and screams, it raised its head, blinking in the sunlight. Roaring, the scaley creature unfurled bat-like wings and took off.

People screamed and fled in all directions, but Donna's supporters remained.

Roberto slipped on a large leather glove as Donna returned to the microphone. "Signor and Signora Alvarez and their son Roberto will enforce my campaign promises. Fire salamanders are fragile beasts who rarely survive outside of their native mountains. The Alvarez family was the first to keep fire salamanders this far north of the equator." She paused for her supporters to applaud. "Don't be shy. Say hello if you see them on the street."

Donna's supporters lifted a banner that read 'Welcome Alvarez Family.'

"Without them, we could not defend our border."

A subtle change in the atmosphere pressed Tonya's eardrums like an increase in pressure. Donna made sweeping gestures sending crystalline sparks over the crowd. It was the same spell Tonya had seen at the parade. Mundanes and Old Families would hear different messages as Donna continued her speech.

"An invisible wall now protects Loon Lake from the Mundanes. Old Family citizens can walk through, but ordinary people won't see the Old Village anymore. In Loon Lake City, they can shop, go to the theater, hospital, or school, while, behind invisible walls, we can practice magic in the Old Village. Let the demonstration begin!"

Cheers erupted from the thinning crowd of Old Family supporters. Most Mundanes had scattered when Mother Dragon appeared.

Roberto lifted a squirming canvas sack and shook it over his head. "Foolish Donna." Roberto's voice purred with sarcasm. "There's no such thing as a fire salamander. Our dragons are the largest in the world thanks to the ambient magic of Loon Lake and my assistant Priya's mystical energy." With a nod to Priya in the crowd, Roberto snapped his fingers.

The dragon flew in slow, wide circles above the beach. The sun gleamed on its slate-blue scales, reflecting sparkling rainbow hues. It was magnificent.

From the bag, Roberto held up an enormous rat. "I love watching dragons hunt."

Tonya stared at Roberto. Was this the same boy who had once fallen for her roommate, Lynette? His smile was as reptilian as the creature's.

"They eat cows and pigs, but keep your children and pets inside." With whistle blasts, Roberto made the dragon fly up the beach. He tossed a live rodent, which the beast snapped up on the flyby. "Two dragons could easily police Loon Lake. If Donna's militia goes over budget, extra guards make excellent dragon food."

His father drew him aside.

"Just kidding. My parents welcome you to a new era of sophistication for Loon Lake with a cosmopolitan attitude."

Donna and her brothers regarded Roberto and family, open-mouthed.

On her next flyby, Mother Dragon glanced at Tonya's pine tree and made eye contact.

Please, please let her keep going.

Mother Dragon screeched, banked sharply, then turned in a wide arc, setting a course for Tonya's tree.

Maybe she wanted to eat another rat snack. Maybe she liked to show off her precision flying skills.

Maybe Tonya didn't have seven thousand pounds of angry dragon coming after her!

58

Crack! The dragon landed on the branch below Tonya.

With a graceful leap, Tonya landed on a higher branch and pulled herself up to the next. The higher she climbed, the closer the next branch, like the rungs of a shrinking ladder.

The dragon's weight bent the treetop horizontally, sending shock waves into the trunk. Branches snapped and fell, showering Tonya with pine needles. She resisted sliding down, but the branch under the dragon bent farther, bringing them eye-to-eye.

A massive paw swiped at her.

She jumped.

"Yeow!" Something jerked her up. Arms and legs dangling, she glanced over her shoulder. The beast had hooked the back of her jeans in its claws. It lifted her closer until the sunlight glinting off its scales blinded her. Toothy jaws opened wide enough to swallow her.

She struggled and punched at the claw suspending her, hoping to tear her jeans. On the beach, a citizen crouched on the sand, aiming a hunting rifle at them.

"Don't shoot!" Tonya waved frantically, but he was too far away to hear.

Tonya?

It was Helen! *Charm the dragon and tell it to let me go.*

As she dangled from the dragon's teeth, wondering if it would drop her to her death, Helen answered in her head. *I'll try, but the Staff of Storms might be too close. It feels like Donna brought it with her.*

Wait, how am I hearing you?

You're my daughter. They can weaken my powers, but at close range, our telepathic link is too strong to break.

Stop the shooter, or he might hit me too.

The dragon leaped skyward and flew toward the island. It flexed its claws which cut through her jeans as if they were tissue paper. Out of telepathic range, Helen couldn't help. Nobody could. Tonya would drown when it dragged her underwater to its nest.

"Hey! Dragon! What do you want?"

In a fairy tale, the dragon would answer, and she could bargain her way out of danger, but it didn't react. Tonya twisted and turned, trying to escape its claws. Pain shrilled and blood wet her back, but she kept wriggling.

"Dragon!" It was stop it or die. She searched her pockets for weapons. Lipstick, a dinner mint, and a key ring with a whistle on it. Tonya blew her lungs empty.

To catch a rising air current, Mother Dragon banked hard. At that moment, Tonya threw the hard candy at its nose. The mint bounced away but, perhaps intrigued by the scent, a prehensile tongue snaked out to probe Tonya for more snacks. This was the tongue that had dragged her under water. Hanging by her belt, Tonya swung back and forth, until, at the top of the arc, she kicked the dragon's jaw.

Its mouth snapped shut and, bellowing, it flew erratically, losing altitude. A long pink tongue segment flew past Tonya's face, sheared off by its razor teeth.

"Cat got your tongue? So much for negotiating." Tonya wound up and kicked its nose.

With a roar, the dragon loosened its claws, sending Tonya into freefall.

59

Hurtling sideways, she hit the water. Skipped like a stone. Sank.

Every inch of her aching and bruised, she kicked to the surface and opened wide for a deep breath—but couldn't inhale. Her brain went into overdrive.

Was she underwater? No?

Was her mouth open? Yes.

Her body kicked and thrashed, which didn't help. Spots appeared in front of her eyes. Her legs lost the strength to kick. If she passed out, she'd drown.

Deliberately, Tonya rolled onto her back and relaxed her chest. Staring upward, she took tiny sips of air, her ribs aching with each inhalation. The impact had knocked the wind out of her.

In the steely sky, the dragon flew a graceful arc, then headed for the beach. Rolling onto her front, Tonya sprinted for shore. Adrenaline powered ten fast strokes without a breath, but the beach was a marathon swim away. The choppy waves might hide her from Mother Dragon, but powering through them was grueling. To make it, she had to pace herself.

The high-pitched whine of an outboard engine alerted her to a boat close by.

"Awooga! Awooga!" Zain waved with one hand on the steering wheel of the supply barge. "You heard me," he shouted. "Awooga!"

As he reversed the boat into place, Priya, Zain, and Grace leaned over the rail waving and calling. Tonya's heart raced with excitement as Drake threw a life ring on a rope.

In three strokes, she grabbed on and let him pull her in. When she reached the gunnel, Drake leaned out and took her hand. With one pull, he lifted her out of the water and into his arms. They kissed and hugged until Drake's shirt front was soaking wet, and Tonya needed to come up for air.

Zain turned the boat and raced for Loon Lake beach. Meanwhile, the dragon changed directions and passed over their heads.

Grace yelled, "Get down!"

Mouth open and talons extended, Mother Dragon swooped overhead. Zain hunkered under the retractable canopy, which the dragon clawed off and carried away.

"Stupid boat. Go faster!" yelled Zain. With the accelerator pushed to max, the vibrating deck tickled Tonya's feet.

Drake's arms around her made Tonya feel safe, but her presence put her friends in danger. Priya showed no fear, and Grace had risked her life to come along. Zain had shrugged off the dragon attack and kept on driving. Unfortunately, Mother Dragon wouldn't relent until she captured Tonya and buried her in the cave. There had to be something Tonya could do, but her powers were gone.

Fortunately, she wasn't the only one with powers.

She joined Priya at the railing. "You created the dragon."

"She's sorry, okay." Zain's hair whipped in his face.

Tonya took Priya's hands. "You created it, so you can stop it."

"I wasn't conscious. It felt like a nightmare when Roberto used my magic to grow his dragons."

"It's your power. You can create anything. Think of yourself back in the studio. Concentrate like when you were sculpting the dragon."

"Maybe it will think you're its mother." Zain called back from the cockpit. "Come to me, dear sweet one. I have a nice ice cream cone for you ... Pow!" He punched the air.

"Try," Tonya said. "What have you got to lose?"

Priya gripped the rail, planted her feet, and closed her eyes. Tonya put a hand on Priya's right shoulder, and Drake did the same from his side.

"You got this," said Grace, who stood with Zain in the cockpit.

A moment later, Zain said, "Nothing's happening."

"Shut up, Zain." Grace poked him in the ribs.

"It's not a statue," Priya sighed. "What am I supposed to do?"

"Anything, but quick!" Zain ducked and let go of the wheel to cover his head with his hands.

"Incoming!" Grace shouted.

Priya held up her hands and screamed, a long wavering cry.

The dragon pulled up short. Instead of attacking, it landed on the stern and poked its nose at Priya, turning its head left and right like a confused dog. Spotting Zain, its expression hardened, and it crept forward, sulfurous smoke escaping its nostrils.

"Hey!" Tonya waved to attract the dragon's attention.

Drake took the wheel.

Slowing, the dragon sniffed the air, turned, and stared at Tonya. Its nostrils flared and tatters of ripped tongue hung out of its mouth as it lumbered toward her.

Backing away, Tonya wedged herself between towers of empty grocery crates. What remained of the dragon's tongue weaved through the gap and wrapped itself around her ankle. She struggled but couldn't break free.

It opened its mouth and breathed fire.

Heat scorched her face, her lungs ... the world.

Explosions dazzled. Overhead, light rocketed in exploding comets of yellow, purple, and red. Priya had transformed the dragon's flame into fireworks. The confused beast sat on its haunches, staring at the sky.

"Thank you!" She wanted to hug Priya, but the dragon's tongue still held her leg. "Anybody got a knife?"

"Don't move." Grace grabbed a hatchet out of the emergency kit and hacked at the tongue until it released Tonya and slithered away.

With a deck-shaking bellow, the dragon took off, circling the boat. Drake brought them close to the pier.

What to do when they arrived? Priya could convert the dragon's flames to fireworks, but what about its teeth and claws? Her friends depended on her, but she couldn't defend them alone. Telepathically, Tonya reached out to find Helen who waited, hidden in a stand of sumac lining the beach.

If we lure the dragon to the pier, can you charm it?

I'll try.

Helen met them at the pier. With luck, Mother Dragon wouldn't eat the person harboring the last of her eggs. Tonya got onto the pier and waved her arms.

"Hey, Spiky Tooth!"

That got the dragon's attention. It swooped down and followed her ashore, tail switching like it was a dog expecting a treat. A hundred yards up the beach, the beast stopped and eyed Tonya warily.

Helen stood very still beside Tonya, concentrating on the dragon.

Slowly, the dragon lowered its forelegs onto the sand and settled its head between them. It was obeying Helen!

A shrill whistle brought the dragon to its haunches. On the beach in front of the pavilion, Roberto held up a rat. The dragon flew over and snatched it from Roberto. When he blew double and triple blasts of the whistle, the dragon obediently changed course and flew toward the island.

With tears in her eyes, Tonya rushed to Helen. "Now, they have to set you free."

Helen opened her arms to hug Tonya. "What's that?" She pointed to Tonya's distended belly.

Tonya explained the origin of the dragon's egg. "Donna took my powers so I can't draw out its life force. Can you remove it?"

"When we defeated Waldock," Helen said, "my power magnified yours, but only you can draw out life force."

Tonya's friends joined them on the beach, and they headed for Helen's car. In the parking lot, Donna, Marta, and a posse of young Mods intercepted them.

Marta smirked. "You're not going anywhere."

Donna pointed at Tonya's belly. "I have your power now, except I don't destroy life. I make it thrive." Life force flowed from the trees through Donna's hands into Tonya's belly.

For a moment, Tonya believed her enemy was trying to save her life. As if. Tonya's belly skin stretched as the creature wriggled and grew exponentially, sending pain shooting through her abdomen. The egg started to crack and deep inside her, something tore.

Tonya grasped Helen's hands. "Please kill it."

"I can't." She charged over to Donna and slapped her before the young Mods could react. "You call yourself a mother?

"Thank you for assaulting me." Donna tapped something on her phone. "Ashton Security is on the way."

"Priya!" Tonya screamed. "Help me."

"What can I do?"

"Suck out its life. Kill it!"

"I only know how to make art."

Marta laughed.

Helen lunged at Donna, knocking her over, but the connection held. The energy flow would continue until either Tonya or Donna died.

Deep inside Tonya, the creature broke out of its shell.

60

PAIN DOUBLED TONYA OVER. "Use your powers, Priya. Change it into something!"

Priya pulled Tonya into her arms. "I'll form a dagger in its heart."

But Tonya felt no change. The thing ravaged her insides, making her head swoon.

Close by, Helen and Donna grappled while the young Mods and Ninjas struggled for dominance.

Priya's voice wavered. "It's not working."

"Pretend I'm one of your sculptures. Let the magic flow through you." Tonya shouted, "Helen, can you amp up Priya's power?"

"Maybe."

Donna leaped at Helen, toppling her.

"Too late," Donna squeezed Helen's windpipe so hard, the effort made veins stand out on her forehead.

"Stop!" Marta hauled Donna off Helen and led her mother away, cursing loudly. Gradually, the Mods stopped fighting and followed the quarreling Ashtons.

Tonya urged her friends into a circle. The Ninjas joined them and linked arms with Priya. Helen limped to Tonya. When they touched, a tickle of energy flowed through the group. Tonya felt the creature inside hesitate, then chomp on her entrails. Her legs buckled, but Drake pulled her into his shoulder and his warmth dulled the pain.

Crunch. Her rib.

Tonya's legs wobbled. "Priya, shape the dragon into something else."

"I can't."

"Mom?" It was the first time Tonya had called Helen that out loud.

Helen smiled at Tonya. "The Staff of Storms siphoned away your magical energy, but it couldn't take all of your ability. Priya has the power, and I'm a catalyst. If we combine forces, we can do this."

"I'm trying," Priya spoke through gritted teeth.

"Close your eyes and concentrate." Tonya moved Priya's hand onto her belly. "Do you sense a green ball of energy?"

"I am so sorry."

Helen opened a psychic connection linking Tonya to Priya, and Drake's love swelled in like a warm cloud, enveloping all three.

Priya's eyes went wide. "I can."

Through Helen's link, Tonya envisioned what she wanted—her body without a parasite. On instinct, the Ninjas closed a protective circle around them. Tonya relinquished control, connected through Helen and Priya.

It seemed to work until a fourth mind bumbled into theirs. Blind and hollow, it was ravenous. When it sensed their presence, it stopped gnawing. Tonya felt its hunger in the darkness and its yearning for the sky. The creature demanded freedom and offered Tonya survival at a price. Its cold intelligence shocked her. Ravenous for life, it left her no other choice.

Helen broke the link first. Had she sensed what Tonya had done?

Had Priya?

If not, she would never tell.

Drake swept her into his arms. "Are you all right?"

Tonya nodded and smiled but didn't cry until they kissed. Salty tears wet their lips, but she never wanted it to stop.

It didn't matter that Donna had won the election. Betty had testified to Mom's innocence in front of the whole town. She had Drake, Priya, Shin, and the Ninjas back. Her heart swelled. With a rich new life ahead, of course she'd survive.

As long as the dragon inside kept its word.

61

Tonya and her friends arrived at City Hall early to save a seat for Helen. Donna had announced the meeting on the Old Family News app, and the gallery was filling quickly.

"Can you believe this decor?" Priya heard about it from the Librarian.

Leveraging the powers of her supporters, Donna had forced City Councilors to cast spells all night to complete the renovation. Combining their powers, they had replaced faded blue carpets with black marble veined in gold and white. Donna's new mayor's desk sat on a raised platform. Carved from exotic woods, it perched on the backs of four ebony panthers showing their fangs.

The meeting was exclusively for Old Families, but Tonya sat with Drake to her left, Priya to her right, and the Ninjas seated in the row behind them. Her Mundane friends deserved to know what was happening.

It had been chaos on the roads that morning, with Mundane citizens driving in circles, looking for locations they couldn't remember. Each Mundane who lived or worked in historic Loon Lake Village suffered from amnesia, which increased as they neared the invisible wall.

Angry Old Family folk packed the gallery. Their Mundane friends couldn't find Loon Lake Village anymore. The wall separated coworkers, friends, roommates, and spouses.

Donna's meeting was supposed to announce new security policies, but people were there to protest. Signs and flags waved throughout the gallery bearing hand-painted slogans like *One Loon Lake for All* and *Give Me Back My Husband!*

One tier below the mayor's desk, councilors filed into rows of seats that faced each other across a hardwood stage. Some elders moved heavily. Others rubbed at their eyes, dark-rimmed from casting spells late into the night. But they filled every seat. Not one dared to be absent.

Donna stood on her special riser, a few steps higher than the councilors. "Look at you, trudging in like sulky teens." She tutted. "Where's your sense of fun?"

Former Mayor Thornton sat near the front of the stage with an oxygen tank beside him. His face reddened. "We see you, Donna Ashton! Without Helen's magic to bewitch voters, you can't trick people anymore."

"Poor Mr. Thornton. Don't wear yourself out." She stared him down. "I think it's time to take your medicine again."

At the back of the stage, Tonya sensed something amiss. Wind swirled like a dust devil. It grew and transformed into a spinning cone of purple sand. Donna turned as lighting struck, tumbling her onto the main platform. Spectators gasped as she struggled to stand.

A long leg thrust out of the fading twister attached to a spry elder in a silk suit. He crossed the stage and stepped over Donna's body before turning to face the gallery. His wrinkles stood like sand under wave action, furrowing his face.

"Greetings representatives of ..." He looked around. "This place."

"Loon Lake." Donna stood and dusted off her skirt.

"No matter. National Council has observed recent events, and we applaud you for finally arresting the correct murderer and pardoning Helen Fitzpatrick. She and her daughter, Tonya, are to be commended for defending the town." With a wrist flick, he sent a burst of magic at Tonya. Her prison anklet clanked to the floor in steaming pieces.

Chatter rippled through the crowd as Drake and Priya applauded. Zain stood and whistled through his fingers until Grace urged him to sit.

Red-faced, Donna leaped to confront the National Councilor, who nodded gravely and lifted his right hand to her in a papal gesture.

There was an awkward pause. Donna bent her neck to kiss his ring. When she straightened, dwarfed by the elder's six-foot-six frame, her mouth opened and closed wordlessly. She waved her arms, put her hands to her face, then raced across the stage.

In front of Tonya's third row seat, Donna stopped. Her mouth opened to scream, but nothing came out.

"What's wrong with her?" Zain asked. "She looks like a landed fish."

"She'll be fine," the Councilor explained. "Over many years, National Council has noticed how loudly local representatives voice their opinions. With thousands of hidden magical communities to manage, we simply don't have time for chitchat. It's better to judge and move on, which brings me to my ruling. Old Loon Lake shall open to the outside magical world but remain secret to Mundanes. It's of no concern to us how local government achieves this."

Grains of violet sand swirled at the back of the stage. "Wait!" Tonya shouted. "Don't go. What about my friends? Make the Ashtons promise not to wipe their memories."

"Very well." He addressed the councilors. "Heal their minds. For their valiant efforts, from now on, you must give them the same rights and privileges as members of your Old Families."

No longer caring who heard, Tonya pleaded, "There's a dragon inside of me. Please remove it?"

A hundred wrinkles deepened when he raised an eyebrow, making Tonya wonder how old he was.

"Dragons are outside my purview."

"Take me with you? National Council will know what to do."

He smiled, flashing sharp canines, and pointed at the gallery. "Voila, the world's greatest dragon specialists. Señor and Señora Alvarez, would you deal with this?"

From her place in the front row, Roberto's mother stood with a motherly smile. "Of course. My dear, I'll take good care of you."

As if. She'd rather face the beast within.

62

A WEEK LATER, TONYA stood atop an enormous boulder on the island facing a boisterous crowd carrying hoes and shovels. Sun heated her ball cap, and her thin t-shirt clung to her newly flattened stomach. Her hasty accord with the beast within had held. The dragon had become part of her, and she had become part of it, so it never needed to eat its way out of her body. As long as Tonya kept their secret bargain, they could coexist, and Senora Alvarez wouldn't have to touch her.

"Go on," Zain urged. "Speech! Speech!"

He was smiling, but Tonya knew how much he hated to wait. Unfortunately, words wouldn't come to her dry mouth. Mom was skilled at public speaking, but Helen was busy addressing her own group in Loon Lake.

Beyond the crowd, blackened stumps poked through soft gray ash like chin stubble. Dragons were responsible, although the desolation reminded her of the ruined cemetery where Helen gathered her crew. Encouraged by Grace's smile and Drake's expectant face, Tonya cleared her throat and took a calming breath.

"Thank you for coming. It's wonderful to see such a turnout. Your enthusiasm took my little tree planting idea and grew it until we have two crews. In the cemetery, Helen leads an even larger group. Today, we plant 1000 trees to restore Loon Lake."

Applause erupted from citizens nearby, Mundanes and Old Families standing together.

"We are all Loon Lakers. Some practice magic, and some don't. You might follow new ways or long for bygone days. Magic has hurt my family, but so have the rules against it. Before we start, I want to thank City Council for ruling justly. Thanks to them, Helen is free and ready to serve her community again."

As the applause grew, Tonya blinked back a joyful tear. She never expected Loon Lakers to embrace Mom or herself.

"Magic goes where it likes and empowers at will. The lines between Mundane and magical families have eroded. Priya can explain it better." She stepped down as her best friend leaped onto the boulder and waved at the throng.

For the occasion, Priya had designed a dress covered in peacocks, inspired by her mother's creations. Her warm smile enveloped the crowd.

"Loon Lake gives magic, regardless of where your ancestors lie. It helped me channel magic into art before I knew what I was doing. My family in Toronto never believed in the supernatural, but in Loon Lake, magic inspires my art and lets me speak to ghosts."

A tall, muscular blonde wove his way to the front of the crowd, distracting Tonya from Priya's talk. Drake vaulted onto the boulder beside Priya, then offered Tonya his hand.

"Drake, would you say a few words?" Priya asked.

Drake stood between the young women with one arm around Tonya's waist. "Priya's abilities saved me from a dragon, and I have an awful lot to live for."

He pulled Tonya to face him, and they kissed to rising applause until, as the kiss deepened, Zain's whistles and catcalls returned them to earth.

Tonya spotted him in the crowd holding Grace's hand. Wait, were Zain and Grace an item now?

From the mainland, Helen spoke in Tonya's mind. *You did it. Marta and the Mods have come to the cemetery, shovels in hand.*

How to reply? The wall still stood, patrolled by Ashton Security. Mother Dragon still lived on the island, although Roberto had promised to control her. Poor Mayor Thornton had recovered, but Donna Ashton was still mayor.

There's still so much to do.

You united this community. For one day, relax and enjoy it.

Thanks, Mom. That never got old.

Priya ended her speech to a round of applause.

The last boatload of volunteers joined them, and Tonya raised her fist. "Let's plant trees!"

Standing behind a row of burlap sacks, Tonya and the Ninjas handed saplings to volunteers. A straw hat shaded one woman's face but her hands looked familiar. Tonya blurted, "Mom?"

Barbara smiled shyly. "Got one of those for me?"

Tonya gave her a sapling, then wrapped her hands around Barbara's. "Does this mean we're good?"

Barbara blinked. Her straw hat bobbed, but before Tonya could say more, her mother turned and melted back into the crush.

On the lake, diamonds dazzled under an intense blue sky. It would heat up later, in time for the community to swim at the beach. They couldn't repair the island forest overnight, and some losses could never be replaced, but together, Loon Lakers were building a new era of growth and peace.

Get your next Loon Lake novel at books2read.com/MaajaWentz.

For free stories and publishing news, join Loon Lake Readers at maajawentz.com.

Author's Note

Thank you for reading *Double Dead Magic*. Members of my reading club, Loon Lake Readers, can look forward to a free mystery novella set in a secret museum for occult Victorian treasures. *Deadly Museum* takes place across the lake from *Double Dead Magic*. Expect hidden vampires, charismatic shifters, and a young museum curator determined to uncover her mother's murderer.

For free stories and new releases, join Loon Lake Readers at maajawentz.com.

Loon Lake Magic Series
Feeding Frenzy: Curse of the Necromancer
Double Dead Magic
Besieged & Bespelled

Besieged & Bespelled

Will the hero become the monster?

Tonya is accused of murdering the mayor by Loon Lake's handsome new paranormal investigator. To prove her innocence, she must solve the crime as Loon Lake copes with an overwhelming influx of spell-casting tourists. When medicine and magic can't cure her, Tonya must deal with her crafty inner dragon. As Tonya's powers grow, her control fades. Can she outwit this new dragon self, or will a good girl start breaking bad?

Get your next *Loon Lake Magic* book at books2read.com/MaajaWentz.

ACKNOWLEDGMENTS

For their encouragement and feedback on the manuscript, I would like to thank Carolyn Charron, Doug Smith, Rebecca Simkin, Melissa Gold, Susan QRose, and Nanci M. Pattenden. For their steadfast support, I would also like to thank Robb Ainley and Heather Ball. From the WCYR and the WCDR, I wish to express my gratitude for my online writing companions Diane Bator, Loni Cameron, Gary D. McGugan, M.C. Perron, Melissa Small, Val Tobin, Les Kerr, Lana Pickering, Maureen Curry, Melanie Dorval, Jennifer Racine, Johanna Harrigan. Chris Szego and Sara Mack contributed valuable professional insights. For their love and support, I am grateful to Gunnar and Thomas Wentz, Ross Banks, Sean and Patricia Banks, Ryan and Vanessa Banks, Ralph and Bonnie Banks, and Doug, Larry, and Lynda Kilpatrick.

ABOUT THE AUTHOR

Maaja Wentz concocts magical worlds and mysteries to tantalize your imagination. Her first novel, *Feeding Frenzy: Curse of the Necromancer*, earned a Wattpad award. Her story, "Inside of a Dog," appeared in *Ellery Queen Mystery Magazine*, which described it as "very original." Maaja works as a teacher-librarian in Toronto, Canada.

Find out more at maajawentz.com.